Tim Heald is an ex-chair of the Crime Writers' Association and a Fellow of the Royal Society of Literature. He is the editor of several anthologies and the Folio Society's four-volume selection of all-time great crime stories. Tim Heald lives in Cornwall.

A DEATH ON THE OCEAN WAVE

Doctor Tudor Cornwall is head of criminal studies at the University of Wessex. Accompanied by his star pupil, Elizabeth Burney, Tudor boards the good ship *Duchess* as a guest speaker on a transatlantic crossing which goes spectacularly wrong. Are the Irish journalists actually terrorists in disguise? Does the captain really have laryngitis? How come Freddie Grim, formerly of Scotland Yard, is preaching at matins? Was the flambé at Doctor and Frau Umlaut's table meant to be quite so explosive? Is Prince Abdullah a real Royal? And, most importantly, can Tudor solve these and other mysteries before the ship docks?

TIM HEALD

A DEATH ON THE OCEAN WAVE

Complete and Unabridged

ULVERSCROFT
Leicester

First published in Great Britain in 2007 by
Robert Hale Limited
London

First Large Print Edition
published 2008
by arrangement with
Robert Hale Limited
London

The moral right of the author has been asserted

British Library CIP Data

Heald, Tim
    A death on the ocean wave.—Large print ed.—
Ulverscroft large print series: adventure & suspense
1. Cornwall, Tudor (Fictitious character)—Fiction
2. College teachers—Fiction
3. Transatlantic voyages—Fiction
4. Detective and mystery stories
5. Large type books
I. Title
823.9'14 [F]

ISBN 978–1–84782–211–6

Published by
F. A. Thorpe (Publishing)
Anstey, Leicestershire

Set by Words & Graphics Ltd.
Anstey, Leicestershire
Printed and bound in Great Britain by
T. J. International Ltd., Padstow, Cornwall

This book is printed on acid-free paper

1

The *Duchess* didn't look like a cruise ship. She had two funnels, round port holes, scrubbed wooden decks and a jaunty air of sea-worthiness which suggested a bygone era in which passengers travelled by sea because that was the best and possibly the only way of getting from A to B. The *Duchess* was all brass, teak and jolly Jack tar. She was the pride and joy of Riviera Shipping, the smartest, most eclectic and most expensive shipping line of the twenty-first century. No bingo and balcony, no chrome and casino: this was P.O.S.H.

Doctor Tudor Cornwall stood on the Budmouth Quayside and sighed. Middle age was making him conservative and old-fashioned. He who had once been an awkward, progressive maverick, castigated by his opponents as a dangerous leftie was now reduced to celebrating the traditional lines of a ship that looked like a ship.

'Nice, eh?' he said to the gamine figure at his side.

Elizabeth Burney smiled. 'Yeah,' she said. 'Sort of thing I used to have in my bath when I was a kid.'

They could have been father and daughter. He, grizzled, tweedy, beetle-browed, over-coated, feeling the cold of a bright, sharp October morning; she, booted, be-jeaned, cotton-shirted, cashmere-sweatered, unbothered by the chill; he, fifty-something; she, twenty-something. But not father, not daughter — guest lecturer; research assistant.

He was looking forward to the assignment. Some people didn't enjoy transatlantics. They were bored by day after day of featureless ocean. The rise and fall of the dangerous deep made them sick and alarmed; consequently they couldn't eat; conversely they drank too much. Tudor, on the other hand, relished the unaccustomed isolation; he liked getting no signal on his mobile; he enjoyed caviar and cold, dry château-bottled Muscadet. Applause was gratifying as well. Likewise recognition. As Reader in Criminal Studies at the University of Wessex, head of an increasingly well-regarded department, author, expert, broadcaster, aspiring television personality, Dr Tudor Cornwall was on the verge of celebrity. Actually, in his own worlds of Wessex and criminal studies he was a celebrity, albeit a minor one. 'Minor' celebrity, he reflected, was a bit like 'minor' poet or 'minor' public school. It was almost a pejorative. Never mind, on the good ship *Duchess* he was a guest lecturer and therefore *ipso facto* a celebrity grade one, alpha male. He was not a vain man but the notion gave a keen edge to his anticipation.

The girl, on the other hand, was just beginning. She was a blank page, the beginning of a book, could go anywhere, could become anything. Not that she was unformed. Far from it. She was a precociously developed personality, smart and streetwise way beyond her years. Tasmanian by birth and upbringing she was as far from home as it was possible to be. An uprooted orphan, she never spoke of family or friends down under. It was as if she had drawn a line under her past, wiped the slate clean, moved on. She herself would never have used such clichés for she was naturally original and inventive. But she seemed to have no past. It was as if she had been beamed in from outer space — which, in a sense, she had.

They had met when Tudor was on a Visiting Fellowship in that far-off land. Even then she had an ambiguous, shady reputation. She was the protégé of Tudor's oldest but false friend, Ashley Carpenter. Probably his mistress, though that was too old-fashioned a word to describe their relationship. She was also alleged to be the college thief, though this, too, was an assumption without serious substance. She had been foisted on Tudor in what, at the time, had seemed like a final act of revenge by Carpenter. Subsequent events had cast doubts on this. Tudor still thought of her as some sort of Trojan horse, but he no longer regarded her as hostile. She seemed well disposed, affectionate even, and she was awfully bright. Although he couldn't admit it, even to himself, he was more than a little in love with her. She, on the other hand, didn't appear to be in love with anyone. She never mentioned Ashley Carpenter.

'Well, star pupil,' said the Reader in Criminal Studies, grasping the handle of his battered leather suitcase, 'shall we go on board?'

She smiled up at him.

'Why not?' she said. 'She's home for a week.'

'Not quite a week,' he said. 'We dock in New York in six days' time.'

She hefted her rucksack on to her shoulders.

'That's hair splitting,' she said. 'I think of it as a week. Call it a nautical week. Like a knot. Chronological equivalent of a sea-mile.'

Her teacher sucked his teeth. 'A week is a week. Six days is six days. You can't have it both ways.'

'I like having it both ways,' she said. 'Suits

my temperament. If I say six days is a week then a week is six days. That's the meaning of meaning.'

'Oh shut up,' he said. 'Stop being tiresome and precocious.'

There were procedures to be gone through. There were, reflected both Tudor and Elizabeth, always procedures to be gone through. This was what so much of life had become: a procedure to be gone through. Tudor's professional life should have been divided into teaching and researching and writing. Instead it was dominated by form-filling and pen-pushing and answering to a faceless, humourless, gormless bureaucracy. Elizabeth's particular bugbear were the immigration authorities who seemed to have an antipathy to Australians in general and her in particular. These were particular procedural problems, but both of them were confronted with the increasing regimentation and regulation of modern life. For free spirits such as them the experience was hobbling. For professional crime-studiers who believed that everything they did should be individual, intuitive, quirky and idiosyncratic the constant drive to make them conform to a grim post-Stalinist pattern of behaviour was a constant reproach. Crime didn't stick to rules. That was the whole point.

The pre-boarding procedures took place in a large corrugated-iron shed cursorily tricked out with tired bunting and frayed red carpet. As formalities went these were agreeably perfunctory. Luggage went through an X-ray screening machine and was then whisked off to their cabins. It was a listless examination as was the body search, performed by bored men and women out-sourced from some private agency and abetted by hand-held metal detectors. Tudor and the girl knew that it was all a charade, a sop to the terror instilled in so many westerners by the destruction of the World Trade Centre. It meant nothing but it made people feel good, or at any rate less bad. It created the illusion that the President of the United States was doing something. Likewise the British Prime Minister. Tudor knew perfectly well, and his talks with his friends and contacts in the Intelligence Services confirmed, that if any terrorist organization worth its salt wanted to do something horrible to a cruise liner it was a doddle.

Nevertheless the two of them submitted to the more or less pointless formalities with a good grace before striding purposefully up the gangplank and submitting their shiny new ID cards to the beaming Filipino purserette at the vessel's entrance.

'Welcome aboard,' she said. The badge attached to her crisp, starched white shirt, said 'Cherry.'

Tudor and Elizabeth smiled back.

Cherry consulted a chart on the baize-covered table in front of her, then turned to a gallery of hooks behind her and picked off two old-fashioned keys with heavy wooden tags.

'Two floors up,' she said. 'Boat deck, aft. Adjacent cabins.'

She smiled with what might have been innuendo but might just have been friendliness.

Tudor and Elizabeth smiled back in a blank semi-expressionless way that ignored any suggestion of suggestiveness, accepted their keys and moved off in the direction of the stairways which were carpeted in blue and lined with photographs and portraits of assorted aristocrats and royals from Britain and beyond. Two decks up they turned left along the *Duchess*'s starboard corridor until at the very end they found their cabins.

'I'd like to be on deck when we sail out,' said Tudor. 'Why don't I see you by the Lido Bar in half an hours' time?'

'Where's the Lido Bar?' she asked, wide-eyed, innocent.

'You'll find it,' said Tudor. 'She's a small

ship. If in doubt ask a uniform.' Tudor had guest-lectured on the *Duchess* before. He knew his way around. So, metaphorically at least, did Elizabeth even though this was her first time on board.

The cabin, like the ship, was old-fashioned. After all, the *Duchess* had been built in Gdansk some twenty years earlier when Lech Walesa was strutting his stuff. Poles were fine ship-builders but, like the Pope and Walesa, they were essentially traditionalist. Thus Tudor's cabin had sturdy mahogany furnishings and a serviceable *en-suite* bathroom but no gold taps and no balcony. Indeed it didn't even have a window but a couple of large, brass-surrounded port holes. Port holes on a modern cruise-ship. Good-selling point, he reckoned.

His cases would come in good time and be stored in the walk-in fitted cupboard. He eyed the half-bottle of champagne on the coffee table and decided to broach it later, then picked up the heavy vanilla envelope with 'Doctor Tudor Cornwall, Guest Lecturer, Cabin BD77' written in inky loops on the outside, and opened it with his fingers, thinking, slightly pompously, that a line of Riviera's pretensions really ought to provide paper-knives in its boat deck cabins.

There was a stiffy inside bidding him to a

Captain's Cocktail Party in the ballroom that evening after they had set sail. He noticed that the Captain — though 'Master' was the preferred moniker — was still Sam Hardy. He had sailed with Sam before. Several times. He must be getting on for retirement age. Not that Sam had much to do with sailing the ship. He was a Captain Birds Eye sort of captain, all jovial bonhomie and silver whiskers, more at home waltzing round the dance floor with elderly widows or telling noon-time jokes over the Tannoy from the bridge. The actual work was done by his officers. Well, that was unfair, conceded Tudor. Being mine host and master of ceremonies on a ship like the *Duchess* was a twenty-four hour permanent smile, constant charm, never-a-cross-word sort of job, and in a way far harder work than actually making sure the old ship got safely from one side of the Atlantic to the other. Tudor wouldn't have liked being master of the *Duchess* but it suited old Sam Hardy. The ladies liked him and that was all that mattered.

There was another envelope, similarly addressed though this time in typewriting.

Tudor smiled. He knew what this was and he smiled as he read it.

'Hi Tudor!' it ran. 'Good to have you

aboard again. I really look forward to more of your criminal experiences and I know the lucky passengers are in for a real treat as usual. We'll be having a short briefing in the cinema at 9.00 p.m. this evening for guest lecturers, gentlemen hosts and other entertainers. And I'd be delighted if you and your companion could join me and the rest of the team for dinner in the Chatsworth Room at 7.30 for 8.00. Look forward to catching up. Best, Mandy xx.' 'Mandy' and the kisses were handwritten and underneath were the words 'Mandy Goldslinger. Cruise director.' He liked Mandy. They, too, had worked together in the past. She was of a certain age and uncertain antecedents: Coral Gables by way of Budapest. She could, up to a point, have been one of the Gabor sisters if life had panned out differently. Her virtues of brash street-wise American pzazz perfectly complimented the stolid all-British joviality of Skipper Sam.

Tudor put the two missives back on the table and contemplated the bowl of fruit: apple, banana, two kiwi fruit, red and white grapes. Standard issue for Guest Lecturer Grade One. He wondered who his colleagues would be, what the passengers would be like. The lumpen passenger list was always pretty much the same. Likewise the lecturers. But voyages such as this invariably threw up the odd surprise.

He was sure this would be no exception.

Thinking which, he picked up his key and set off in the direction of the Lido Bar, whistling a happy tune.

2

Tudor was not a sailor in the practical sense of knowing a quarter deck from a poop or being able to tie a sheepshank or a bowline but he took a real pleasure in things nautical. It was a vicarious spectator's pleasure but none the less genuine for that. Watching the *Duchess* cast off her chains before being tug-nudged gently out to sea was always mesmerizing. He had little real understanding of what was happening, but he derived an expert's enjoyment from watching other experts at work. You didn't have to be C.S. Forester or Patrick O'Brien to do that.

The ship's orchestra, all seven of them, were playing 'When the Saints Go Marching In' from a balcony on the deck above and white-clothed trestle-tables were laid out with canapés and bottles of sparkling white Spanish wine.

Tudor took a glass of Cava and a miniature chipolata on a toothpick, walked to the rail and contemplated.

The members of the band seemed even older than the passengers. They had a slightly louche, left-over air that Tudor associated with a certain sort of seaside resort or spa. People who he'd assumed were long dead turned up in resorts such as Budmouth, or ships such as the *Duchess*, all wrinkles and hip-replacements. Many of them were orphaned so that one was likely to encounter Gerry without the Pacemakers (now there was a sick geriatric joke), Wayne Fontana without the Mindbenders or Brian Poole without the Tremeloes. Ancient has-beens strutting their last at the end of the pier. At least the *Duchess*'s orchestra had each other, wearied by age though not yet quite condemned. They played the 'Saints' with a lugubrious panache, their moustaches improbably dyed, their paunches straining against the buttons of striped pseudo-Edwardian waistcoats, wispy hair lapping discoloured collars. They might, reflected Tudor, have known better days, they might have been drowning but they were still playing on. Dying but not dead, bloodied but unbowed. In a moment they'd do 'Land of Hope and Glory'. At least the ship's orchestra was maintaining a pretence and doing so with conviction.

This was not always the case with the passengers who in some cases closely resembled what Tudor imagined were the walking dead. Watching from the rail, drink

13

and sausage in hand, he had a sense that he was the only man alive. This was unfair. He knew it as soon as he thought it. There were some sprightly nonagenarians tripping the light prosaic before his eyes on the lido deck. Men and women were mocking age and infirmity, shaking their zimmers at the Grim Reaper and embarking with stoicism and gritted teeth on what for some was almost certainly the Last Great Cruise.

One or two had already changed for dinner: men in white tuxedos with brightly coloured waistcoats and cummerbunds, buckled shoes, sleek silver hair and gold fillings; women in long ball gown concoctions that would not have shamed Barbara Cartland and beehive hair-do's that suggested a golf-club dinner-dance in Surrey circa Coronation Year. Tudor told himself to stop being ageist and snobby. He himself wasn't that smart nor that young any more. Those still in day clothes had an air of *Carry on Cruising*: male tattoos of a bruiser, sergeant's mess quality Hawaiian shirts, golf shoes; sandals with knee-length socks, pearls, cardigans. Everything said money and middle Britain; Thatcherland; suburban and provincial. 'Shut up,' Tudor said to himself. 'This is your audience. If you want to be a celebrity you've got to make people like this like you.' Even as he said it, half of him at least thought the game not worth the candle.

'Doctor Cornwall,' said a smoky estuarine voice at his elbow, 'nice to see you again. Muriel and I wondered whether you might be on board.' When Tudor too obviously didn't recognize him, he said, 'St Petersburg the year before last. Freddie Grim, ex-Flying Squad. Used to work with Slipper of the Yard.'

'Of course,' said Cornwall, suddenly remembering all too well. Slipper was the man who had developed an obsession with the Great Train Robber, Ronnie Biggs. Freddie Grim had been close to him. If Cornwall's memory was not playing tricks Freddie Grim had accompanied Slipper on the notoriously unsuccessful trip to Brazil where they had so ignominiously failed to secure the robber's extradition.

'Great Train Robbery,' he said hopefully and was relieved when Grim's mouth cracked in a satisfied grin, revealing a set of unnaturally even teeth and letting out a halitosis breeze of stale tobacco and lunch-time beer. He was wearing a blazer with the badge which appeared to be that of the Metropolitan Police Bowls Club and a matching cravat.

'Spot on,' said the former policeman. 'See

our Ron's trying to get let out on compassionate.'

Biggs was in Belmarsh prison where he was supposed to have suffered a couple of strokes. His solicitor was having no luck at all in presenting his client as more sinned against than sinning.

'Giving us the *Bounty* again?'

Tudor nearly always did his 'Mutiny on the *Bounty*' talk on board ship. In it he proved beyond reasonable doubt that Captain Bligh was strict but fair and that his survival in a small open boat was due to consummate seamanship. It seemed an appropriate subject for a cruise and invariably proved popular. His audiences tended to sympathize even if they felt Bligh's rules were strictly administered. In fact, *particularly* if strictly administered. Most of them were almost certainly floggers if not hangers. Probably both.

'You remember Muriel,' said Grim, indicating a small, mousy woman at his side, who smiled and seemed embarrassed.

'Of course,' lied Tudor. Muriel was infinitely forgettable and looked as if she knew it. Her husband did not exactly cast a long shadow but it was long enough to render Muriel effectively invisible.

'Hope we don't have a rough crossing,' said

Muriel's husband. 'Muriel's not the world's greatest sailor, are you, pet?'

'To be honest,' she said, 'I'd rather be at home with the cats. But Freddie says you're only young once and travel broadens the mind.'

Grim seemed pleased to be credited with such an original thought.

'What do they know of England, I always say,' he said, unexpectedly, 'who only England know?'

Tudor nodded sagely and was rescued by the arrival of Elizabeth Burney who had not changed for dinner and was still showing no sign of feeling the cold. Not even a goose bump.

'Elizabeth is my research assistant,' he said. 'She's doing a criminal studies Ph.D.'

It was disconcerting to see that the Grims didn't believe him. Their hand-shaking and smiling were polite but incredulous. Almost immediately Freddie and Muriel moved away on the pretext of more food and drink. Cruising, even aboard as serious a ship as the *Duchess*, was unhealthily often about more food and drink.

'You want to know who's top of the bill speakerwise?' asked Elizabeth, sipping her wine and gazing appreciatively at the rippling, tattooed muscles of burly stevedores doing serious stuff with crates and ropes.

'I thought *I* was top of the bill speakerwise, as you so charmingly put it,' said Tudor, smiling at her in protective mode.

'Well, I'm afraid Sir Goronwy Watkyn's on board.'

Tudor almost choked on his Cava.

'You're joking,' he said, when he'd done some dramatic coughing and throat clearing, 'Not that fraudulent Welsh goat? And I suppose that means the ghastly Myfanwy's on board, no doubt with her bloody harp.'

Actually the ghastly Myfanwy never brought her own harp but commandeered the instrument belonging to the ship's harpist. This inevitably caused grief and allegations of broken strings. She was a rotten harpist but fancied herself on account, of course, of being Welsh. As for her husband, Tudor loathed him with a passion. He was famous for a series of fantasy-style detective stories set in some Tolkien-like Middle Kingdom full of monsters and wizards and featuring a Grand Bard of the Gorsedd who was the first of the great detectives. In Tudor's estimation they were utter tosh but they had made Goronwy Watkyn millions of pounds and earned him a knighthood for 'Services to Literature.' When he was not writing about his ridiculous bard he wrote a series of gritty contemporary police procedurals set,

Tudor thought, in Aberystwyth, or it might have been Bangor. These featured a detective called Dai Jones and were written under the pseudonym J.P.R. Morgan. It was all complete rubbish. Watkyn liked to use his title, habitually wore canary-yellow ankle socks and an overly neat goatee which waggled ridiculously when he talked — which was incessantly.

'You've just ruined my trip,' said Tudor almost meaning it, 'And who in heaven's name do you imagine the bloke in the white robe is? The one with the harem in attendance. Surely he shouldn't be drinking alcohol? Not in that outfit!'

'He's called Prince Abdullah and beyond that we know practically nothing whatever except that he's paid in full and the money's good.' The speaker was a blue-ish blonde with vivid make-up in a silk kaftan slit oriental style virtually up to the waist. The heels of her shoes were ridiculously high, especially for being on a ship, and she jangled with bangles. Tudor suspected, but didn't know for sure, that the rocks on her rings were real.

'Mandy!' he exclaimed, kissing her on both cheeks. 'Mandy, this is Elizabeth Burney, my star post-graduate pupil at the University of Wessex, who's come along to help out. Elizabeth this is Mandy Goldslinger, the fabulous Cruise Director of the good ship *Duchess*.'

'*Enchanté*,' said Ms Goldslinger extending a hand with astonishingly long almost witch-like fingernails painted in gilt-flecked purple.

'Hi,' said Elizabeth.

Tudor could have been mistaken but the encounter did not somehow suggest love-at-first-sight. Inside his head he heard the all-too-familiar clinking of ice cubes.

'I hope you've run the appropriate security checks,' said Tudor, not joking.

'Oh you crime people!' said Ms Goldslinger, loudly enough to make some adjoining passengers turn round curiously. 'That's exactly what that cutie, Goronwy Watkyn said. You're all the same. Too too paranoid.'

'You can't be too careful,' said Tudor. 'You know how vulnerable cruise ships are to international terrorism. They could be kamikaze-wives. Has anybody looked under their jellabas?'

'Tudor darling,' said the cruise director, 'Prince Abdullah is a hundred per cent kosher. I personally have checked with my dear friend Eddie Mortimer who does communications for Kofi Anan at the United Nations and he tells me that the Prince has a great humanitarian record and is a prominent

20

member of the Yemeni royal family.'

'The Yemenis don't have a royal family,' said Elizabeth, 'it's a Marxist republic.'

'Oh Yemeni shemeni,' said Mandy. 'The Prince wouldn't hurt a fly. Matter of fact hurting even flies is against his religion. He's a sweetie.'

'You'll be sorry if they've all got bombs in their shoes,' said Tudor. The ship's orchestra had not moved on to 'Land of Hope and Glory' but were playing 'Hearts of Oak'. Tudor reckoned they were in for a good half-hour of songs nautical and marine.

'Who are those two sitting on thrones?' he asked, noticing a man in a safari suit with a much younger blonde wife. They were both smoking and sitting in upholstered chairs. Although not actually behind rope or barbed wire they looked as if they had been cordoned off from the vulgar herd. They had their own table with their own cloth, their own canapés, their own bottle in their own ice bucket.

Mandy frowned.

'Those are the Umlauts,' she said. 'They think they own the ship. Trouble is they more or less do.'

'Expand,' said Tudor. 'I don't understand.'

'Oh shucks,' said Mandy unexpectedly. She took a long swig from her glass and wiped her brow. On the shore and the lower decks, dockers and seamen were doing really serious things with ropes, chains and hawsers. They were cutting the remaining umbilical links between the *Duchess* and Budmouth. Slowly but unmistakably the ship began to move away from the quayside. Her siren sounded. The band was playing 'A Life on the Ocean Wave.' Passengers were leaning over the rails and waving at anyone they could see on shore. Some shorebound onlookers waved back. Others maintained an air of stolid indifference. Tudor felt oddly moved. He was pleased that Elizabeth seemed to share his elation to the extent even of waving at a couple of stout workers on the quayside. They waved back cheerily.

'Umlaut takes the Imperial Suite for at least six months of the year. He treats the ship as his office and home. He makes his own rules. He does deals with Zurich and New York and the City and Tokyo and the Middle East.'

'What sort of deals?' asked Tudor, only half paying attention.

'Money,' said Mandy. 'Money, money, money. Mrs Umlaut, Frau Umlaut, is dripping in diamonds, festooned with fur and treats everyone on board as if they were personal staff. Mr Umlaut, Herr Umlaut, Gottfried to his friends — if he had any — is rude beyond belief, tells the captain what to do, makes the rules as he goes along, believes that money can buy anything and anyone.'

'They don't sound altogether attractive,' said Tudor.

Mandy Goldslinger looked thoughtfully across the broadening band of murky water which now separated the vessel from the United Kingdom.

'I could cheerfully murder the Umlauts,' she said. 'I really could.'

3

Entering the ballroom for the welcome party was like coming on to the set of a modern-dress version of *HMS Pinafore*. Tudor half expected the ship's officers lined up in white and blue with gold braid on their wrists and shoulders to launch into a chorus of 'He's hardly ever sick at sea/ so give three cheers and one cheer more/ for the hardy Captain' and so on. The stagey impression of faux-seamanship took its cue from the Master himself who was, naturally, first in line. Captain Sam, universally known, for obvious reasons, as 'Kiss me Hardy' was straight from Central Casting. The skipper had what the Royal Navy refers to as a 'full set,' meaning a moustache and beard. These were white in Santa Claus style. Indeed, if one could imagine Father Christmas in the uniform of a Merchant Navy captain you would have a pretty good idea of what Captain Hardy actually looked like for he was a big, pink-faced fellow who shook like jelly when he laughed which was often. He didn't actually bellow out 'Ho, ho, ho!' or even

'Yo, ho, ho!' but you would not have put it past him.

The Master recognized Tudor and greeted him cordially enough though with less joviality than he managed for complete strangers.

When Tudor introduced Elizabeth Burney, Hardy called her 'Little Lady' which was a big mistake. The Master was excellent with women of advanced years and preferably limited intelligence; the younger and brighter they got the less at ease he seemed. Despite the fact that he exuded a sort of mariner's braggadocio which suggested — was designed to suggest — extreme virility, Tudor had doubts about his true sexuality. Helped out at tea parties, if you asked Tudor. Not that Tudor had the slightest objection to men who helped out at tea parties. Some of his best friends came into just that category. But he was uneasy with pretence, uncomfortable with deceit. After all it was part of his trade and he, as much as the next man, disliked mixing business with pleasure.

The canapés and Cava had been moved from the lido deck to the ballroom with the Riviera Line's customary expedition and lack of fuss. The ship's orchestra had, however, been replaced by a female duet playing 'Greensleeves' on classical guitar and cello.

They looked Baltic: high cheekbones, possibly deceptive innocence, elegant but cheap strapless dresses, probably fresh out of the conservatoire in Riga, Tallin or Vilnius.

Tudor and Elizabeth negotiated the line of immaculate, beaming, hand-shaking ship's officers; avoided having their photograph taken, took a gesture of food and drink and headed for a far-off corner of the room from which better to survey the crew and crowd.

'Is it always like this?' the girl asked, looking around wide-eyed yet not innocent. They were out in the English Channel now and there was a breeze. Force Three perhaps. The curtains of the ballroom, tasselled purple, swayed gently and so did some of the passengers. It would be rougher before they reached New York. It always was and despite the ship's sophisticated stabilizers it would keep a lot of paying customers in their cabins. It seemed an expensive way of making yourself sick.

An elderly man in a white tuxedo, a spangled turquoise cummerbund with matching made-up bow tie, and sleek white hair, shimmered over.

'Doctor Cornwall,' he said proffering a much-ringed hand, 'Ambrose Perry.'

'Ah,' said Tudor, medium-term memory

working overtime. 'Ambrose Perry, the gentleman host.'

'That am I,' said the over-groomed old gent in a curiously archaic and unconvincing turn of phrase which suited his general demeanour and appearance.

Tudor remembered that Mr Perry had once owned and run a hairdresser's salon in Bromley called, he thought Daphne's. He was a brilliant gentleman host: attentive, unthreatening, with a mean fox-trot and a devilish paso doble. In the afternoons — or *après-midis* as he described them — he called bingo or played bridge. He also picked up gossip like nobody's business. Gentlemen hosts aboard the *Duchess* were privy to more secrets than the barmen.

'Prince Abdullah *and* the Umlauts,' said the host, 'that's a double whammy we've never seen before.'

'Is that a problem?' asked Tudor, all *faux-naïf*.

'Problem?!' exclaimed Mr Perry, 'A 'many-pipe problem' as your Sherlock Holmes might have said. Herr Umlaut and the Prince are not exactly bosom companions. And the accommodation question is unanswerable.'

'How do you mean?' asked Elizabeth. She had no idea what he meant.

'I mean,' said Ambrose, a tad stuffily, 'that

on most of the *Duchess* voyages either the Herr Doctor or the Prince travel and that invariably they do so without the other. Never the twain shall meet. However, on this occasion they have been, as it were, double-booked. And alas, there is room, accommodationally speaking for but one top banana on board.'

He spoke a very strange English. Both Tudor and Elizabeth independently supposed that he must originally have come from somewhere else.

'Surely you can have as many top bananas as you like?' said Elizabeth.

'There is only one Imperial Suite,' said Ambrose. 'On voyages when the Prince is on board without the Umlauts he is always given the Imperial. So he is used to it. It confers status. Unassaillable status. On those occasions when the Umlauts are on board without the Prince it is they who are installed in the Imperial. They, too, are used to it and they, too, enjoy the status. The Imperial comes complete with a butler whereas the likes of you and I have to make do with bowls of fruit.'

Tudor suspected that gentlemen hosts probably had to share cabins with each other. In the complex hierarchy of life aboard the *Duchess* a guest speaker ranked higher than a gentleman host by several degrees. Guest speakers were among the elite of the non-paying passengers though, Tudor conceded, some guest speakers were more equal than others and he had a horrid feeling that, at least in the eyes of the Master and the shipping line, he was out-ranked by Sir Goronwy Watkyn. He was afraid Watkyn would have the better cabin.

'So you're saying that whoever gets the Imperial Suite is universally acknowledged to be Top Banana.' Elizabeth was catching on fast, as usual. 'And on most voyages there is no contest but that on this occasion someone has to decide who gets it and the verdict went to the Umlauts . . . ' She paused for thought and then said, 'Who decides? They presumably don't just flip a coin?'

'It would be the Master's judgement that decided,' said Perry, 'Everything on board ship is down to the Master. He is indeed *master of all he surveys.*'

'But surely,' said Tudor, 'that sort of thing is decided by the company? And it depends on how much money changes hands?'

'Maybe,' said Perry, 'maybe not. I think the Captain's word is final. What's more I'm fairly certain that's how the Prince and the Umlauts would see it.' And he shimmered off in the direction of the dance floor whence duty and some very old women were beckoning him to do something appropriate with the last of the remaining light fantastic.

'What an odd bloke!' said Elizabeth when he was out of earshot — not far, as he was obviously acoustically threatened despite being hearing-aid-enhanced. Deaf as a post notwithstanding the pink plastic stuffed into his right ear.

A waiter came past with a tray of drinks and Tudor and Elizabeth both exchanged empty glasses for full.

'You do need to pace yourself on board ship,' said Tudor, in headmasterly mode. 'Sometimes you feel there's nothing to do except eat and drink, especially on transatlantic runs.'

Swilling and browsing seemed pretty pervasive except for the small knot of old people gliding about the dance floor. Cello and classical guitar made an unlikely dance band but some of those on board had the sort of itchy feet which would have bopped to Beethoven or charlestoned to Chopin. These were serious dancers and although in conventional pedestrial mode many of them would have been stiff to the point of virtual paralysis, they seemed when dancing to glide as if on ice. The pair from the University of Wessex watched with admiration and disbelief.

'Och, Dr Cornwall,' said a broad Scottish voice which was almost as much of a stereotypical Scottish voice as the Captain's was a bucolic English one. Actually, thought Tudor, Scots, even caricature ones like this, never quite said 'Och' but it was a reasonable Sassenach rendition of the noise a Scot makes at the beginning of his first paragraph.

'Angus Donaldson,' said the uniformed figure who boasted a ruddy wind-burned face and a set of whiskers almost as full as the Captain's. His beard and moustache, however, were as black as the Master's were silver. He looked about twenty years younger. 'We sailed on the *Baroness* a few years back. Sardinia and Sicily as I recall. You mounted a spirited defence of Captain Bligh in your talk on the *Bounty*.'

'He'll be doing it again,' said Elizabeth flirtatiously and Tudor introduced her.

'You were Master of the *Baroness*,' said Tudor, tentatively.

'Aye,' said Donaldson. 'She was a grand wee vessel. I was very happy with her, but, as they say, you have to move on, draw a line under things, so here I am on the flagship of the fleet.'

'Forgive me,' said Tudor, squinting at Donaldson's gold braid stripes, 'But what's your title here?'

31

'You mean, why am I not captaining the ship?' He laughed, though not sounding wildly amused. Then he lowered his voice. 'I'll let you into a secret,' he said, 'when it comes to actually sailing the ship, that's the responsibility of the Staff Captain and the Staff Captain is yours truly. The Staff Captain is by way of what on dry land would be called the Chief Executive or perhaps the Chief Operating Officer. The Master would be the Chairman or the President. He's the senior officer but he doesn't actually *do* a great deal.'

Tudor wondered why he was telling him this, perilously close as it was to insubordination. He hardly knew the man.

Staff Captain Donaldson obviously noticed Tudor's surprise.

'Don't get me wrong, Doctor,' he said, 'Sam Hardy's a fine man and a grand sailor in his day and in his way. I'm not saying his position is purely cosmetic but, well you know how it is. Being the life and soul of the party and a convincing figurehead is a full-time job of its own. It would be asking too much to expect him to steer and navigate as well.'

'Quite,' said Tudor, bearing in mind the old adage about ceasing to dig when you'd created a deep hole.

They were saved from further embarrassment by Mandy Goldslinger ringing a handbell.

'Hi, ladies and gentlemen, girls and boys,' she shouted. 'Welcome aboard the good ship *Duchess*. I'm your Cruise Director Mandy and we're going to have ourselves a ball together during the next few days. However before we do it's my wonderful job to introduce our wonderful captain so that he can introduce y'all to his wonderful crew. I know some of you have sailed on this great ship before and so you'll know what a truly great captain we're privileged to have at the helm. Those of you who are on board for the first time are privileged to have the opportunity of finding out what true captaincy really is. So without more ado, let me present the finest skipper on the seven seas, the pride and joy of Her Majesty's Merchant Navy, the one and only, irreplaceable, irresistible Captain Samuel Hardy.'

Saying which she set down her bell on the table at her side and clapped her hands in a vigorous invitation to everyone else to do the same. Behind her on stage the ship's orchestra who had reappeared as if by magic played a few jaunty bars of 'Rule Britannia' and the Master, preening his elegant moustaches in a gesture which not even the simplest passenger could have mistaken for modesty, acknowledged the plaudits of the multitude before gesturing for silence, as if the applause was all too much for him.

'Welcome, ladies and gentleman, to the finest ship afloat,' he began and continued in a spirit of effusive bonhomie for a minute or two before introducing Staff Captain Donaldson, the Chief Engineer, the Purser, the Head Housekeeper, the Executive Chef and others, all of whom smiled and waved and were rewarded by enthusiastic clapping and even the occasional unexpected wolf-whistle.

Finally, when he had done, the Master raised his glass, and said, 'As they say on the other side of the English Channel. *Bon Voyage*! I wish you all a calm passage and a safe arrival in New York City.'

Tudor shrugged at his pretty protégé.

'Tempting fate a bit wouldn't you say?' he asked softly.

'I'd say so,' she replied. 'What do you imagine the captain said to the passengers when the *Titanic* set sail?'

'Much the same, I imagine,' said Tudor.

'You bet,' she said.

4

Elizabeth Burney shivered on the spiral staircase leading to the Chatsworth Restaurant and pulled her Tasmanian Trefusis stole tight about her shoulders.

'I feel like I'm in the cast of an Agatha Christie. *Murder on the Nile* maybe,' she said. 'Is it always like this?'

' 'As if', not 'like' if you don't mind,' he said pedantically.

'Oh, for f***'s sake,' she said, 'Can you do content not context and answer the question?'

Tudor winced. He knew he had fuddy-duddy tendencies.

'Cruise ships are natural settings for Agatha Christie type mysteries,' he said, in pedagogic mode. 'In some respects you could argue that the modern cruise ship is the conscious equivalent of the twentieth-century house-party. Or at least that's what it aspires to. Equally you could say that ships like the *Duchess* are deliberately trying to ape the great transatlantic passenger liners of the same period. The passengers reflect this. So yes.'

'So yes,' she mimicked, giggling lightly, 'it's like being on stage for a matinée of *The Mousetrap*.'

'Yes,' he said, 'I know what you mean. Cruising's a bit like that.'

She giggled again and was still smiling when they entered the dining room which was doing its best to live up to its name. Seeing the pastiche oil paintings on the panelled walls Tudor remembered a quip about a Duke of Devonshire at his stately pile selling off old masters to pay for young mistresses. These paintings were ersatz old masters unlike the real duke's paintings in the real Chatsworth and like the room itself they were part of a charade or pantomime. This was part of the essence of cruising. The experience involved a voluntary suspension of disbelief. For the duration of the voyage passengers entered a world of fantasy and make-believe. For most of them this was entirely agreeable. For some, some of the time, it was not.

This was now the case for Dr Tudor Cornwall who found himself obliged to dine at a table for four with Sir Goronwy and Lady Watkyn. This was Tudor's idea of purgatory. Sir Goronwy droned on through the prawn cocktail, droned on through the brownish steak Diane, droned on through the

Black Forest gâteau and droned on through the coffee and petits fours. Whenever the drone seemed to stop in order to allow the speaker a pause for breath, Lady Watkyn managed to get in a sycophantic coda which prevented either Tudor or Elizabeth putting an end to what represented the verbal equivalent of a record-breaking marathon snooker break.

In one way or another Watkyn droned on about himself. As a professional Welshman he possessed all the verbosity of the most long-winded Methodist preacher but without the redeeming belief in the Almighty. As far as Sir Goronwy Watkyn was concerned there was only one God and that was Sir Goronwy Watkyn. He would have said that his conversation — he would never have accepted that it was actually a monologue — ranged far and wide. In a sense this was true for, beginning with crime fiction, its origins, its history, its current strengths and weaknesses he rabbited on through politics from his own parish in the Marches just outside Montgomery, to Welsh politics — with special reference to the Plaid — British politics, European politics and global politics. He could do terrorism, cricket, crochet, crosswords. You name it. His knowledge may not have run very deep but it ran impossibly wide. And every topic he covered had an ill-concealed subtext which was, of course, Sir Goronwy Watkyn. You might think that, for instance, he was delivering a detailed and dispassionate account of British military operations in Iraq, but before long he himself would make an entrance. Sometimes he would appear as a name-dropping British Council lecturer, sometimes as a military expert who had done national service in the Royal Welch Fusiliers; sometimes as a young man who had once canoed up the Euphrates, perhaps as an author who had once set a novel in Biblical Babylon. It was, in Tudor's opinion, self-opinionated and self-obsessed tripe. Impressive in its way, rather like a model of the Empire State building made entirely of matchsticks, or the world's biggest Cornish pasty, but tripe nonetheless. The dreaded Myfanwy's breathy little encomia filled the tiny silences like the pitter-patter of confetti. 'So right, darling . . . so very, very right . . . that was the time the Prime Minister phoned to ask . . . Watty's laver bread is the best in the whole of Wales.' And so on.

It was said of him that if he simply dropped God's name then all was normal. Thus when Sir Goronwy confided, 'I was walking down to the club and happened to bump into God. Had a most interesting chat,' that was OK.

The time to worry was when he said, 'I was walking down to the club when I bumped into Goronwy Watkyn.' That was when you knew you were in trouble and Goronwy was due for one of his periodic periods in the bin.

After a while Tudor started to play a game of guessing how many times the old wind-bag would use the words 'I' or 'me' in the next five minutes. The incidence of both was astonishingly high and increased noticeably in proportion to the ingestion of alcohol which was itself significant. Riviera Shipping might have been conservative on the food lines but it was generous with the claret.

Mandy Goldslinger was at a table with two gentlemen hosts and the Baltic classical guitarist. They seemed to be having a much better time than the Cornwall-Watkyn table. There was evidence of four-way conversation, story-telling, jokes and even laughter. The two boys and two girls of the celebrity, all-singing, all-dancing, all-smiling cabaret team of whom no one on board had previously heard, were evidently enjoying an incestuous luv-in. Mandy's deputy, an androgynous wet-behind-the-ears Yorkshire tyke, was hosting a ventriloquist, the water-colour teacher and the computer lecturer. And so on. There were about thirty diners in all.

Just as Tudor was floating into a Goronwy-induced miasma of total inattention and ennui he heard a Watkynism which brought him suddenly back to something approaching life.

'Blah . . . blah . . . Goronwyblah . . . bach . . . hwyl . . . aberblah . . . blahgynolwyn . . . blah . . . watkynblah . . . last voyage of the *Duchess*.'

Tudor reacted like a schnauzer stung by a wasp.

'Last voyage of the *Duchess*?' he repeated, fumbling his way out of half-asleep.

'Last voyage of the *Duchess*, boyo,' said the Welsh knight, taking a long sip of the Australian sticky with which Riviera Shipping had rounded off their largesse. 'The old girl's swansong. At least the last voyage in these particular colours. Dare say she'll re-emerge as a hospital ship for the Swiss Navy or a nautical knocking shop for the dictator in some banana republic. Or a Central African kingdom. There's a public-school educated emperor with a lot of wives in Equatorial Bongo-Bongo land who might just about fit the bill. In any event' — he sipped again, fleshy lips kissing the glass with an almost lascivious caress — 'it's the last time you and I will tread the boards of these particular decks.'

'Are you sure?' asked Tudor, experiencing a frisson of anticipatory alarm. He was beginning to have a bad feeling about this trip.

'This Oz Auslese is warming to the cockles of my old Celtic heart,' said the theatrical old crime writer. 'Sure? Nothing's sure in life. That's the only certainty about our drab existence wouldn't you say? Dylan Thomas has a memorable passage about madness and sanity, but alas I've forgotten it. Ah Dylan, Dylan. How I miss the dear darling boy . . . '

'I remember the line perfectly,' said Tudor, sharply, for he was vexed.

Sir Goronwy shot him a threatened look from under beetling white eyebrows. The eyes were unfocused in a fuddled fashion.

'How did you know?' he asked tetchily.

'One does,' said Tudor, matching the older man's bad temper with his own. 'And how come too that you knew that this was the *Duchess*'s last voyage with Riviera?'

Sir Goronwy smiled elliptically.

'As you suggest,' he said, 'there are things that one simply knows as if by osmosis, picked up on the ether, plucked from the wings of gossip, born to one's ears on the silvery threads of ethereal whispers from one knows not where.'

'Someone told you late one night and

41

you've forgotten who,' said Tudor.

The old fraud was not to be easily riled.

'I never reveal my sources save in works of genuine written scholarship,' said Sir Goronwy. 'In verbal communication seldom if ever. Confidences are not to be betrayed but evidence must be acknowledged. My dear old father, the Reverend Ebenezer Watkyn of Abergynolwyn, of whom you may have heard me speak, was a past master of the telling reference, the learned footnote, the bibliophiliac bibliography, in short of knowledge lightly worn yet properly acknowledged.' He paused, breathless at last and waved at a passing waiter for more dessert wine.

'Ebenezer, Goronwy's da, was a fine man,' said Lady Watkyn, quick as a flash, 'And a wonderful preacher. Held his congregations in the palm of his hand he did, just as if they'd been a lump of dough and they about to be baked into a loaf of bread and fed with the fishes, just as the Good Book tells us.'

It was apparent to Tudor and to Elizabeth Burney that Sir Goronwy was not the only Watkyn the worse for wear alcoholically speaking.

Tudor was wondering whether to go through the charade of intelligent conversation when the Cruise Director shimmered across clanking with costume jewellery and gleaming all over.

'Dahling,' she said breathily, 'would you mind playing musical chairs so that I can sit with these gorgeous people?'

Elizabeth Burney regarded this as a virtually divine intervention and did as she was asked with an alacrity which might have been considered impolite even by the stone cold sober. Sir Goronwy and Lady Watkyn however seemed barely to notice but just continued their seamless droning duet. This was, reflected Tudor, as dispassionately as he was able, a remarkable conversational accomplishment — the sort of thing that ought to go into the *Guinness Book of Records* alongside Gyles Brandreth's longest ever after-dinner speech.

'What's all this,' he hissed, ignoring the Welsh, 'about the *Duchess* being sold? On her last voyage in Riviera colours I'm reliably informed.'

'Reliable, sweetie?' Mandy Goldslinger smiled a sceptical smile implying that this was not even mere gossip but a positive untruth. She could have been right for there was not much to do with Riviera Shipping that Mandy did not know. Cruise Director was a title that did her far less than justice.

'It came from the horse's mouth,' said

Tudor. 'At this very table. Sir Goronwy himself, no less.'

At the mention of his name the Welsh knight came to an unprecedented pause and the slack of his jaw was not, for once, taken up by his harpist harpie wife.

'You're not taking my name in vain I trust. Very verily, all is vanity,' he said theatrically and evidently rather pleased with a joke which only he and his wife seemed to understand.

'Not in the least,' said Tudor pleasantly. 'I was simply confirming with Mandy here what you told me earlier about this being the last voyage of the MV *Duchess*.'

'I always think of the dear thing as the RMS *Duchess* though I suppose she carries no mailbags these days,' said Sir Goronwy. 'The Royal Mail in any case no longer being as regal as it was in the days when the postman rang twice and always came on time. New Labour is little more than republicanism in sheep's clothing though the concept is insulting to sheep, which is as sacred to my nation as the leek or the daffodil.'

Some of Tudor's best friends, Tudor reflected, were Welsh. Indeed as his name suggested he had plenty of Celtic blood himself. He did not, however, wish to claim kinship with the Watkyns.

Mandy Goldslinger cut through this Celtic cackle like a knife through low cholesterol health spread.

'If Riviera are selling,' she said with an air of ill-defined menace, 'then who, I would like to know, is buying? Riviera, as you know, is owned by Atlantic and Pacific, which in turn is owned by Galactic and Global which means, effectively, that there is no one else in the market.'

Sir Goronwy smiled saliverly.

'I'm told that the two most likely purchasers are both on board,' he said, 'and already at daggers drawn. It wouldn't surprise me if we had some dramatic events to entertain us before we arrive in New York.'

He gave a knowing wink and a portentous belch and seeing that his glass was empty rose unsteadily to go in search of a refill.

5

They had a good day in Cork.

Had Tudor been a more flippant, Wodehousian figure, he might have described it as 'an absolute corker' or 'jolly corking run-ashore,' but being the man he was he simply said, that evening when they were back on board nursing a couple of Boris the Barman's lethal but delicious cocktails, 'I rather enjoyed today.'

Elizabeth, who was beginning to read her supervisor as well as he would like to think *he* read *her*, said succinctly, 'Me too.'

Until a few months earlier she had barely been out of Tasmania and then only to the Australian mainland and, just once, to New Zealand on a hiking holiday. Coming to England she had been amazed at how like her own homeland it was, despite being on the other side of the planet. She knew the history and understood how the affinities had arisen but she was nevetheless viscerally amazed at having travelled so many thousands of miles to end up, nearly, exactly where she had begun.

Yet as she settled in she found that the

superficial similarities of cricket and culture, custom and convention were exactly that — superficial. There were profound differences of language and idiom; a pervasive defeatism where she had grown up with optimism and the idea of 'can do'. She felt she had grown up in a place which lived outdoors and where anything was possible. Now she was in a country with low horizons where there was nearly always some sort of bureaucratic regulation that prevented you doing anything interesting or unusual.

She loved being in England because of its complexity and its history. Life in Wessex, even at its not particularly good university, had a texture that was missing in the breezy, nonchalant, new land of her youth.

And now Ireland. She had been told that Cork was not the true Ireland but that it was a place apart: *Corcaigh* — she was irritated by the Gaelic sub-title to everything from road-signs to picture postcards especially the curlicued typeface which she thought pretentious and naff. This didn't stop her and her boss buying postcards — views of tiny typical whitewashed cottages with donkeys. They wrote messages on them for folks back home in a dark pub where they drank cold black Guinness and marvelled at the efficacy of the recent smoking ban which seemed to have been obeyed with remarkable un-Irish alacrity. The juke box played fiddle and squeezebox folk songs of vaguely Republican sentiments. Afterwards they moved to a brighter less sepulchral pub and lunched off big meaty mutton chops and colcannon with more Guinness to drink followed, greatly daring, by an Irish coffee heavily impregnated with Tullamore Dew and with the cream correctly unwhipped and poured over the back of a silver spoon so that it sat fat and mildly yellow on top of the Guinness-black coffee. After lunch they visited St Fimbar's Cathedral which seemed like the rest of the city familiar and yet stridently un-English, then took a cab back to the ship, nodding and smiling uncomprehendingly at the driver's travelogue and what sounded like a long, gloomy weather forecast.

It was oddly reassuring to be back on the *Duchess*. Already she had taken on a familiar home-like quality even though she was no more than a floating hotel. It was part of the attraction of cruising that the ship took on an almost protective coccoon-like air so that after the adventures of a day in some foreign port (well, actually as often as not, seen from the synthetic safety of a chaperoned tour bus) one could relax, feel pampered and unthreatened. Travel without danger, holidays without fuss.

Supplies and fuel had been taken on board in the Irish Republic and so too had passengers. Elizabeth got talking to a group of new arrivals in the bar while Tudor toyed in a desultory manner with the *Irish Times* crossword.

Presently she rejoined him.

'They're a press group,' she said. 'Their leader seems to be a PR person called Jeffrey who could be English, but all the others are Irish and seem to have names beginning with F. The blokes are called Finn, Flan, Fergal, Fingal and even Fimbar and the hackettes have names like Fiannula or Fenella or Felicitas.'

'That sounds like a nun,' said Tudor.

'Doesn't look like a nun,' she said. 'The whole lot are straight out of central casting. Boozing and betting people and they talk funny.'

'I can guess,' he said, 'and what are they here for?'

'Classic freebie,' she said. 'They all, more or less seem to have commissions from Irish papers and magazines. Do you really think there's such a thing as the *Tipperary Tatler*? One of the Fiannulas says she's doing a style piece for them.'

'Anywhere can have a *Tatler*,' said Tudor, caustically. 'Most places do. It's a licence to print money. Even in Tipperary they'll pay money to see if Finn and Flan are sharing a quiet joke over a pint of Guinness in the Fiddler's Flea. Or whatever. *Tatlers* are just parish magazines with ball gowns and black ties. Upwardly mobile gossip.'

'Well,' said Elizabeth thoughtfully, 'Fiannula, or one of them, is doing a style piece for the *Tipperary Tatler*. The other Fiannulas are writing the same sort of drivel for the same sort of non-publications. So are the Finns and the Fimbars. All a complete waste of time and money. They're only here for the beer.'

'And the fruit machines,' said Tudor. 'Oh, and all the romance that goes with a life at sea. They'll write bland complimentary pieces and they'll appear in their publications with bland, complimentary photographs and everyone will be happy.'

'Is that the way it is?' she asked.

'That's the way it is,' said Tudor. 'Way of the world. Nothing really what it seems. All make-believe. Pay enough money and you can make anything happen. Or appear to happen.'

'You don't believe that.'

'I believe that's how it would be if it weren't for people like me. Like us.

Whistle-blowers. The incorruptible.'

The girl stared moodily into her drink and said nothing.

After a while Tudor sunk the last of his cocktail and said, 'Come outside. I think this should be a rather spectacular departure. It usually is. I did it once in the *QE2*. Breathtaking.'

It took a lot to take Elizabeth's breath away but the Irish leave-taking came close. It was dusk as they sailed down river, past the twinkling lights of Cobh and the fairy-tale silhouette of the cathedral and it was as if the whole of Ireland had turned out to wave them on their way across the Atlantic to what so many Irish people regarded as new Ireland across the water where the Irish could be free from the English yolk and your Kennedys and your Reagans walked tall and inherited the earth.

And the Irish lined the waterfront in their smart French, German and Italian cars and they sounded their horns and they flashed their lights and they cried out in the lowering dark and the passengers on board the *Duchess* waved back and some of them smiled, and some of them called back and some of them wept a little for it was all quite magical in a Gaelic way and they stayed on deck until the last winking shaft of light from the beacon on the ultimate cliff disappeared into the evening fog and the ship was truly on her own, utterly so, without land or escort, destined for thousands of miles of dangerous and desolate ocean before they came to the land of the free.

'Time for dinner,' said Tudor with an Englishman's tin tongue.

'You go,' she said, 'I'll catch up.'

He waited a moment, then saw that she really did want to stay and savour the moment. As he walked towards the door that led indoors, he glanced back and saw that she was leaning on the rail gazing down on the white wake gleaming in the dark below. As the ship gathered speed the foaming fan grew more turbulent stretching out in a giant V astern. A handful of gulls still followed them wheeling and mewing before they turned back to the safety of dry land and left the little vessel to the mercy of the ocean. You could almost be forgiven for thinking anthropomorphically of the *Duchess* as she seemed to lengthen her gait and began to stretch out to the even marathon runner's stride which would, in a few days, God willing bring her safely to port.

She was pitching and rolling now as the sea buffeted her and the more she moved the noisier she became. Tudor could never work out whether the rattling and whining of a ship at sea was protest or pleasure but he found the noise oddly comforting — the regular thump of the engines, the sigh of the wind through wire and rigging, the plangent rasp of rivets and plates. This, after all, was what the ship had been built for and she had made countless voyages such as this. The knowledge was reassuring though the future was, as always uncertain.

It was an oddity of all journeys, he reflected, glancing up at the sky which had cleared to reveal a full moon and a Milky Way, that they were at the same time similar yet unique. Each time he took the train from Casterbridge to Waterloo he passed through the same countryside, the same towns, the same stations. Often he showed his ticket to the same guard, smiled a silent greeting to the same passengers, bought coffee from the same girl in the buffet. Yet all these people like himself were older every time, a step or two nearer death, a page or so nearer the end.

Crossing the Atlantic was more glamorous than travelling from Wessex to London and yet the voyage contained the same elements of routine and surprise. Once on board they would all fall easily into observing the fixed points that each person created — meals being pre-eminent but lectures and film shows and bridge sessions all playing their part so that in a way life on ship was almost dull, particularly if you were seated at a table with the Welsh Watkyns.

And yet no two voyages were ever quite the same. However many times the *Duchess* crossed from Britain to America there were always moments of the unexpected to chip away at monotony. Mostly the deviations were trivial, unnoticeable even. Drama was not something the cruise companies encouraged and on the whole they were successful in lulling their customers into a sybaritic somnolence undisturbed by anything untoward.

Tudor spent several moments hesitating on the deck thinking these thoughts, lost in reflections of self-indulgent banality even though they had to do with such fundamental and universal questions as the meaning of life.

He was so abstracted that the sudden opening of the door took him quite by surprise though he realized as he jumped that it was ridiculous to find oneself discomposed by the sudden opening of a door. That was what doors did after all. They opened and shut. Even on board ship. And he was silly, too, to be surprised by the figures who emerged on to the moonlit deck. He would have expected them to have been safely ensconced in their suite, the three waiting hand and foot on the one.

'Good evening,' said Prince Abdullah politely, as he led his three wives into the bracing night.

Tudor inclined his head and said 'Good evening' back. The Prince spoke the greeting like an old-fashioned Englishman, public-school educated, BBC-modulated. Just the tiniest trace of a foreign inflection. The eyes of his wives looked out at Dr Cornwall, the rest of them concealed in jellabas and yashmaks.

He wondered what they were thinking and continued to do so even as he perused his menu at the dinner table a few moments later and considered the great questions which dominated life on ship: whether to have the pâté or the soup; the duck or the beef, whether to drink white or red.

He didn't even notice that the Watkyns were not with him.

6

Tudor was woken by noise in the middle of the night.

For a moment he felt hopelessly, helplessly disoriented as one does when woken suddenly and unexpectedly between alien sheets. It was a klaxon. Deep disorientating noise of an indeterminate character, the sort of thing you'd use on torture victims in Guantánamo or the Lubyanka. Noise so penetrating that it had an almost physical character. It hurt.

Seeing the mahogany panelling, the port hole and his towelling bath robe slung across the end of his bed, feeling the regular sway of his room and hearing the throb and mutter of the vessel's nuts and bolts he quickly remembered where he was. The noise was the blast of the ship's klaxon, usually sounded only as a test or the prelude to the mandatory boat drill.

Seconds later it ceased. A series of metallic clicks followed and then a female voice spoke.

'Good morning ladies and gentlemen,' it said, pleasantly and with a soft Irish lilt which could under other circumstances have seemed quite beguiling. 'We're sorry to have disturbed your sleep and in a moment or two we'll let you resume your slumbers. This is simply to tell you that the ship has now been taken over by the People's Liberation Army of United Ireland. There will be a further announcement in due course but for the time being we ask everyone to remain calm and to stay in your cabins. As far as we can ascertain there are at present no passengers in public areas of the ship. If there is any passenger away from their cabin we ask them to return there. If anyone is found outside their cabin we cannot be responsible for the consequences. However, if everyone stays in bed and goes back to sleep you may rest assured that you will be perfectly safe. Thank you for your attention.'

There was a click and the Tannoy went dead. Tudor switched on the bedside light and looked at his watch. 4.30. The chances of any passenger being up and about, even an insomniac fruit machine user, were remote. It was the best possible moment for a take-over. He rubbed his eyes and considered his position. Any ordinary sensible passenger would do as asked and stay put. Going back to sleep might be a tall order but it was certainly the sensible course of action.

He had doubts, however, whether he was

an 'ordinary sensible passenger'. As a guest speaker his role was ambiguous. He was not an ordinary passenger, but he was not a member of the crew either. Did that confer obligations? How, he wondered, would Sir Goronwy Watkyn react? And there was the added complication, was there not, that he, like Watkyn, was an expert on crime. If, as it appeared, this was an act of piracy, a maritime hi-jack, then this was as much of a crime as the Mutiny on the *Bounty*, on which, he remembered with a start, he was due to speak later this morning.

He was about to decide that going back to sleep would be a dereliction of duty when his phone rang.

It was Elizabeth. The Irish People's Liberation Army might have performed the revolutionary's text-book first task of commandeering the radio station, but they clearly hadn't disabled the communications system. Passenger was still able to talk unto passenger.

'What did you make of that then?' she asked, obviously excited.

'Shhh,' he said nervously and a touch theatrically. 'You don't want someone to hear.'

'Oh come on,' she said. 'Someone is far too bothered trussing up the captain and officers, making sure the crew don't stage a counter-attack. They're not going to bother with cabin-to-cabin communication. They've got other things to do. I think it's my gang though. The so-called Irish travel hacks. I told you there was no such thing as the *Tipperary Tatler*. That was Fiannula on the loudspeaker system.'

'You sure?'

'Pretty sure,' she said.

'Are you surprised?'

He could almost hear her thinking down the line.

'Surprised but not surprised,' she said.

She was good at ambivalence. Properly expressed it carried academic conviction. Certainty was risky. It was fine if you were right, but mistakes were very bad. Bets, she reckoned were, on the whole, better hedged. On the one hand, on the other hand, might end up as a drawn match but it was better to share the points than earn none.

'So what should we do?' asked Tudor.

'We?' she asked. 'What's this *we*, Kemo Sabe? I see no *we* I'm a mere menial. I do as I'm told.'

This was being economic with the truth but at the moment it suited her and it was true that she was, technically, the led and he the leader. He taught, she learned. She sat at

59

his feet, at least as far as the casual observer was concerned. The reality might be different, but she was not going to let on, at least when it didn't suit her.

'You're the boss,' she said. 'I'm staying in bed till they sound the all-clear.'

'OK,' he said, not feeling remotely OK. 'I'll call you after the all-clear.'

He put the phone down.

She was right. It was disconcerting that she was so often right. She was younger than him. And a girl. On both counts she should have been wrong and yet she wasn't.

He lay back and sighed.

'Am I man or am I a mouse?' he asked himself, not sure whether it was a rhetorical question, whether he had the answer, whether he cared, whether he knew, whether, well, anything really . . .

'Man or mouse,' he said out loud. 'Discuss.'

It was a question that had bothered him almost all his life and was doing so now with increasing frequency. It disturbed him in the dark and silent small hours when one was particularly prone to doubt and loss of confidence. In youth he had been relatively confident of his manhood but as the years passed that confidence evaporated. He had read in one of the colour magazines only a week or so earlier that a man's testosterone disappeared faster and faster after the age of something like eighteen. Not that testosterone had ever been his sort of thing. If anything he had always cultivated a sort of refined femininity albeit on the uncompromisingly masculine grounds that girls seemed to like that sort of thing. The Morgan motor car was an exception, he supposed, but that had come relatively late in life and was deliberately designed to compensate for the rodent attacks on his virility. Anyway even the Morgan was a subdued symptom of blokeishness. A hardcore *Maxim* reader would have opted for a Harley-Davidson.

He shook himself. Only a mouse, he told himself, would behave like this. No proper man would conduct such a private conversation at a moment of crisis. It was pusillanimous prevarication. Cometh the hour cometh the man should have been his rallying cry. Not cometh the man cometh the mouse.

He considered his options. Option A was to turn over and go back to sleep. That was the extreme-mouse solution — white mouse tending to albino. The pink-eyed way out. In any case even if he took this cowardly way out it wouldn't work properly because he was far too tense and excited to go back to sleep. The nautical motion of the old ship might be soporific, but the apparent terrorist hijack was far too bracing for even a drowse or a day-dream.

Option B was to get up, have a shave and a shower, dress and be prepared for the terrorists' next move. This was more seductive than A if only because it gave him something to do as well as affording him more time to think. He had to admit that it was still pretty mousy behaviour but on the other hand he would present a tougher, more effective proposition if he were scrubbed up. Also it didn't represent a complete campaign, just part of it. A necessary prelude you might say. Option B might be mouse-like but it could quite easily slip into something altogether more manly. He decided to leave the problem as a straight choice between A and B, leaving consideration of C and possibly further letters of the alphabet until later. He had always admired Fabius Cunctator more than Hannibal. There was a difference between bravery and bravado.

The shower was hot and the shave close. He had, as usual brought his own soap, brown Pears in a box, and he applied shaving soap with an old Trumper's brush with genuine bristles removing it with a new Gillette blade in a safety razor. He quite liked the idea of an old-fashioned razor which you sharpened by stropping, but he was anxious not to appear too much of a fogey. Indeed for someone who gave the impression of not caring about his appearance he cared very much indeed. He believed that such deceptive nonchalance had to be worked at.

As he washed and shaved himself he considered his next move. Yet again he shrank from the really serious decision by just considering what he should wear. If he were going to indulge in serious counter-terrorist activity he would need to convey gravitas and authority. That meant a collar and tie. The tie should definitely not be Channel Four Newscaster with its mutton-dressed-as-lamb garishness but something plain and sober. Not club or old-school-striped which would be unacceptably Fogeyish. He had a green number with white polka-dots which would just about do. Also a plain creamy yellow shirt with gold monogrammed cuff-links. Dark-grey worsted trousers and a dark blue jacket more in the style of an Ivy League reefer than a British blazer. Blue socks and a pair of dark-grey loafers he had picked up in a closing-down sale in a small shoe-shop behind the Frari church in Venice.

When he had packed himself into this outfit he contemplated the result with a satisfaction verging on the smug. He was weathering well, he told himself, and he looked as if he was at the very least a head of department, which indeed he was. It was an image which, he reckoned, inspired respect if not exactly awe. Even Irish terrorists would think twice before tackling him. He looked the sort of man policemen might still, even in the early twenty-first century, call 'Sir'.

Wondering whether the bags under his eyes indicated wisdom or fatigue, the crow's feet healthy scepticism or unhealthy late nights, the flecks of grey at the temple seniority or senility, he found the mouse reasserting itself. There was something wrong with the picture in front of him and he knew that it was a question of conviction. He might have fooled other people into thinking that this was a commanding presence but he didn't fool himself. Not for a minute. He knew that the Tussaud-like image really was just a waxwork façade. He longed to be able to snuff out candles with the flicker of an eyelid at forty paces, but he knew deep down that he would melt at the strike of a match.

He sat down heavily on the bed. Option B was now complete. It was too late for Option A. It was time therefore to consider C and any alternatives he could bring to mind. C was confrontation. If he adopted it he would leave his cabin, walk to the bridge and command the hijackers to put down their weapons and submit to his citizen's arrest.

C for crazy. Even if he were a cross between James Bond and Spiderman this was a really bad idea. If the terrorists were even half serious they'd shoot him on sight. Of course they would. That's what terrorists did. It had happened time and again during his lifetime and before. Moreover, having spent a lifetime studying crime in all its aspects he knew this better than most. The ordinary bloke who 'has a go' is a certain suicide. He might make an adulatory obituary in the next day's paper but that was all.

Option D was to sit down and read a book. Another mousy idea but safe and sensible. He could phone a friend. That meant Elizabeth in the cabin next door but what good could that do? For different reasons he couldn't involve her in either his cowardice or his riskiness. The one would be too embarassing and the other, well, ungentlemanly. In a curious old-fashioned way, he rather cared about that.

He was still wrestling feebly with these choices when his phone rang.

He picked it up and realized that the necessity of making a choice had been removed. The decision was being made for him.

The voice was familiar.

And Irish.

7

'Doctor Cornwall?'

'This is he,' he said, wishing he wasn't.

'You're wanted on the bridge.'

'By whom?' Tudor was surprised by the bolshiness in his voice. If the person to whom he was speaking was the person he thought it was, asking questions, particularly in that tone of voice, was risky.

'Us,' said the voice with Celtic ambiguity. 'We'll send an escort. They'll be with you presently.'

Tudor shrugged. No question now of his sitting in the cabin and reading a book. He wondered what they wanted from him and whether heroics would be required. If he had been seriously contemplating such a course of action he felt somewhat thwarted. A potential initative had been removed. Had he come bursting on to the bridge unannounced he would have held the upper hand. Surprise was a key element in conflict of any kind. All the manuals said so.

Presently there was a sharp knock on the door. The knock had an unpleasantly peremptory quality. It was not a question expecting the answer 'no' nor even entertaining the idea. More of an affirmation of authority.

'Come,' said Tudor, using the expression and the tone of voice he assumed at home in the university when one of his students came calling.

The door was unlocked despite the advice to bolt it while asleep. Tudor had an aversion to locked doors even though it made him vulnerable. It was now flung open with abrupt violence and a stocky figure in a balaclava helmet and combat fatigues stood in the doorway, beckoning. The knocker's left hand held what looked like some sort of pistol. Although firearms came within Tudor's area of knowledge, they were not a speciality. Whatever the man held it gave off an air of metallic menace. The person had not spoken but it exuded male body-language and, more potently and convincingly, male body odour. Strong pong of beer, tobacco and unwashed armpit.

It said nothing but jerked its right hand in an uncouth beckoning fashion while the left pointed the gun barrel at Cornwall's midriff. Compliance seemed desirable even if mousy. In any case Tudor was curious. He had never been involved in a nautical hi-jack before. It would prove an invaluable teaching tool as well as a terrific subject for future cruise lectures. Reasoning thus he did as he was gestured. He was good at rationalizing weakness.

The hijacker shoved him roughly to one side, shut the door and prodded him in the small of the back with what Tudor took to be his gun barrel. Activated in this crude manner he walked.

They went as far as the elevators, ascended three decks to bridge level, exited, walked to a door marked with a red skull and crossbones and words 'Danger. Crew only!' translated into French, Spanish and some script which could, to Tudor, have been Japanese, Chinese or any language from east of Suez. Passing through was the nautical equivalent of going through the green baize door in a stately home which separated upstairs from downstairs, ladies and gentlemen from maids and players. The contrast between passenger accommodation and crew quarters was almost total. Carpet became lino; chandelier, neon strip; polished mahogany, raw steel. In a single second one went from pampered indolence to forced labour. Tudor tried, vainly, to remember the lunar astronaut's oracular words about the instantaneous step for man and mankind but only found himself wondering whether the crew slept in hammocks. It would be difficult to find such anachronistic class distinctions on dry land.

Tudor was thinking of all this in a dreamy academic sort of way when he suddenly realized that he and his demon prodder had emerged on to the bridge. 'Bridge', like so many words on board ship, was misleading for in no way did the area in which Tudor now found himself resemble a structure traversing a road, railway or river. Much less a game of cards. This dimly lit room with its flickering screens and panoramic, wrap-round view of the moon-lit ocean deep was a nerve-centre or control-room but in no recognizable way a 'bridge'. It took him a blinking second or so to accustom himself to the dim half-light and even then he saw only through a glass darkly.

There were five officers on watch. At least that was what he assumed the ghostly white figures to be. He could not make out their features, or their badges of office but their white uniforms glowed in the gloom. Each one of them was being shadowed — literally — by a darker person whom Tudor took to be one of the terrorist team from the Emerald Isle. This was all the hijackers had had to do — break on to or in to the Bridge, commandeer the *Duchess*'s public address system — the maritime equivalent of a banana republic's national broadcasting centre and post office — and Bob's your uncle, the revolution's triumphed and the regime is toppled.

The gorilla-guerilla escort prodded him towards a diminutive shadow which looked female and in charge. These were difficult things to assess in the crepuscular light but Tudor guessed that it was Fiannula or Ffion or whoever the girl from the fictitious *Tipperary Tatler* was and that she was the ring-leader and also the voice who had spoken to everyone over the ship's public address system.

'Doctor Cornwall,' she said in a voice that confirmed that she was a girl and also the voice on the Tannoy. Her air of authority was sufficiently obvious for him to think that his intuition about being the boss was also correct.

'*Tipperary Tatler*,' he said, hoping to fit the last piece into this little jigsaw. It sounded the sort of name Ian Fleming might have given a Bond girl.

'Very astute, Dr Cornwall,' she said, in a brogue so husky and Gaelic that he felt sure it must have been fake. No real Irishwoman would speak like that. It was like something from *Father Ted*, 'I know you're a professional,' she said, 'it's why we asked you to

71

step up here. We're keen to have a plausible mouthpiece.'

'What exactly are you playing at?' he asked, feeling like the mouse that roared, a frisson of daring translating into courage. Yet the remark didn't, he felt, require real courage because, he sensed intuitively, that this was just a game. These people weren't real.

'We're not playing at anything,' said *Tipperary*, lilting. 'This is no game. You'd better believe it.'

'Listen,' said Cornwall, 'it's easy to do what you've done so far because that's the way civilized societies are. We don't live in a police state. Not in Ireland. Not in the UK. Not in the United States. And most certainly not on board an ocean liner such as this. Everything is based on tolerance and trust which means no obtrusive security devices, no armed goons patrolling everywhere, no CCTVs, nothing to make people scared or tense. If you go on holiday you don't expect to end up in Guantánamo. And the only way one can prevent people like you doing what you've just done is by creating a world that is simply not acceptable. Being civilized opens the way for the uncivilized.'

'I agree. Western society is soft, vulnerable. We've just demonstrated that.' She sounded, thought Tudor, more than slightly mad. But you'd have to be more than slightly mad to do what they'd just done.

'You do realize,' said Tudor, 'that what you've done is easy because those in charge have no choice but to make it easy. The reason it doesn't happen more often is that real professionals understand that the only part of an operation such as this which is viable is phase one. The deterrent lies in the certainty of effective response.'

'You're the expert,' said the girl. 'That's why you're here.'

'You could have commandeered Sir Goronwy Watkyn,' said Tudor, playing for time.

'He's fiction,' she said, 'we deal in fact. We also think he's yesterday's story. And a windbag. We know your stuff, Dr Cornwall. You'll do. You suit our purposes perfectly well.'

'Thank you,' said Tudor, 'I'm flattered.'

He was too, up to a point and in a manner of speaking. It was always good to score points over his old crime writer rival even in dodgy circumstances such as this and the circumstances couldn't get much dodgier. Here he was, ivory-tower man, effectively the hostage of a gang of fanatical Irish terrorists on the bridge of a hijacked cruise liner in the middle of the Atlantic Ocean.

In theory he should have known exactly

how to behave but, he had to concede, theory was what he knew about and this, disturbingly and threateningly, was the real thing. It was 'Who wants to be a Millionaire?' syndrome. Any fool could answer Chris Tarrant's patsy questions when they were sitting in an armchair in the comfort of their own home, preferably with a hot milky drink and a packet of chocolate digestives or Jaffa cakes to hand. Plonk them down on one of those uncomfortable stools in the studio under the full glare of the studio lights and the deceptively amiable quiz-master himself and all was utterly different. The mind went blank. One no longer knew what two and two equalled, let alone what the capital of French Equatorial Africa was or who invented the kitchen scales.

'You're not meant to be flattered,' she said. 'Like I said, we deal in facts. You're our man, Dr Cornwall. You're part of the deal. We didn't pick our ship or our cruise at random. We wanted the *Duchess* and we wanted you. An expert on crime. Academic. Cutting edge. The sort of guy Jeremy Paxman would invoke in a crisis. Larry King even. Someone who will play well on the airwaves. Also help us in other ways. You play ball with us; we'll play ball with you.'

Tudor found himself levitating. It had

happened to him once or twice before on the rare occasions when he had found himself in an unaccustomed or threatening session. There had been one such moment when he was summoned to 10 Downing Street for what sounded like a routine consultation with a Whitehall committee of jobsworth bureaucrats only to find himself alone on a sofa with Tony Blair. And another when he agreed to address a meeting of Animal Rights Activists and found himself not, as he had expected, a neutral imparter of inside information, but a target, an enemy alien, a subject of verbal abuse which threatened to teeter over a brink into something more physical. It didn't quite, but he was glad to escape unscathed. On another occasion he had fallen out of a boat off the Cornish coast and had five minutes of thinking he was about to drown.

All three times he had enjoyed what he could only describe as an 'out-of-body-experience'. It was if his soul or brain, (call it what you like depending on the state of your beliefs and he being cheerfully agnostic simply wasn't sure) had left his body and settled at a point a few feet above his head. From this vantage point the thinking part of his being was able to make a far more rational assessment of the situation than if it had remained at head level. The one common factor was that the disembodied regarded base camp with a mixture of disdain and hilarity. From six feet above his head Dr Tudor Cornwall looked, regrettably, a trifle absurd.

It was the same now except that in this case the other principal figure cut little more of a dash than Cornwall. It seemed from on high that the girl was all mouth and no knickers as they say on Tyneside. She was bluffing.

It was all very well knowing this in theory, quite another to act on it. Spaceship Cornwall beamed the message down to base but it was quite another matter for base to act on it.

Cornwall found himself running through his internal 'man or mouse' routine once more. 'Man' would have called the bluff; 'mouse' would have played safe and gone along with the implausible manner and the gun-barrel pointing at the small of his back from an unnervingly close distance. He had a choice and very little time to make it.

'The weapon,' he said, in a voice which was far firmer than he felt, 'which your friend is pointing at me in such a threatening and, if I may say so, melodramatic and superfluous a fashion, intrigues me. I don't think I recognize it. Not, I think, a Mauser or a Walther and certainly not a Smith & Wesson.

I doubt it's Czech or Russian. Beretta I somehow doubt. Chinese perhaps. I don't think I've seen anything quite like it before.'

He was bluffing himself. He knew next to nothing about firearms. In theory maybe, but certainly not in practice. Motivation was his forte not the crude business of execution. He was not a Ludlumite as in Robert of that ilk who devoted whole pages to the minutiae of small-arms.

'How should I know?' asked the girl. 'I leave that sort of thing to others. I do brain not brawn.'

'The truth,' said Cornwall, 'is that you haven't a clue, because' — and here he surprised himself as much as everyone else in the room, by spinning round deftly and grabbing hold of the menacing barrel — 'it isn't a real gun at all.'

8

He was right. It wasn't a Smith & Wesson. Or a Beretta. Or a Walther or Mauser. In fact it wasn't any sort of gun, just a crude piece of make-believe, a piece of black metal piping taped to a roughly hewn wooden butt. It was enough to deceive a startled innocent on a dark night, especially if the owner was wearing a balaclava helmet and combat fatigues. As a blunt instrument wielded with force and precision it might have maimed or even killed but as deployed here on board the *Duchess* it was just a piece of play-acting.

For a moment there was silence.

It was the girl who broke it.

'We didn't want anyone to get hurt,' she said. The words sounded lame.

Tudor turned back to her.

'Oh really,' he said. 'Can't you do better than that?'

A further silence followed. A mid-Atlantic stand-off. Tudor couldn't help feeling rather pleased with himself, but at the same time horrified at what might have been. His alter-ego, that disembodied part of him which had been hovering above his head but which now seemed, mysteriously to have returned to base, had given the correct advice but it was reckless and dangerous counsel. How could it have known? Did it know? Had he acted on a certainty or a desperate hunch. Should he be dead? Was he really a man? Or was he just a mouse in man's clothing? These worries pounded away at him as he tried to concentrate on the immediate issue and maintain his imitation of Action Man, Bond, the cutting edge rather than his preferred mode of cerebral onlooker.

Eventually he said, 'I think you and I had better sit down and have a little chat.'

To his gratification and, once more, surprise, she agreed at once.

There was a room off the bridge, a curious sort of R and R place with a couple of beds, a coffee-maker, some armchairs and a general slightly desperate air of getting-away-from-it all-but-only-just. It was somewhere for those on watch to take forty winks when the situation allowed. A halfway house.

They sat down in two chairs facing each other and said nothing. It was thought-gathering time before the match or the duel or whatever sort of competition this was going to be. Chess? Poker? Tennis? Fencing? Pistols at dawn? Tudor ran through the metaphors and remained unsure. All he knew was that this was adversarial and tricky. They didn't know who was going to lead the first card, make the first serve, take strike. He almost felt like tossing a coin.

'You going to keep that balaclava on? I know what you look like. There's no need to hide.'

She seemed to think about it, then removed the woolly disguise and flicked her head like a dog after a swim. Thick auburn hair bounced down to her shoulders. She was freckled, high cheek-boned, would have been attractive but for an off-putting set of the jaw, an air of fanaticism bordering on madness. Or was Tudor fantasizing? Maybe she just looked a bit silly.

She still said nothing, waiting for him to play a second card.

'So what on earth is this all about?' he said, trying to sound grown-up without being pompous, and not sure he was succeeding, 'What are your demands?'

'It's not as simple as that,' she said, scornfully. 'You know that.'

'Maybe,' said Tudor, 'but if we're going to negotiate, we need to have some sort of agenda. We can't negotiate nothing.'

'What did you have in mind?' she asked, sounding almost as if she meant it.

'Oh come on.' Tudor's exasperation was

genuine. 'You're the one who's hijacked the ship. Terrorists have causes. That means reasons, demands. You've effectively taken us all hostage so you have to come up with terms. You release us in return for . . . well, in return for whatever it is that you want.'

'Who says so?'

'It's the convention.'

'We don't believe in convention. That's why we're here.' She flicked her head back, thrust out her jaw and challenged him to argue. 'Suicide bombers don't make demands,' she continued. 'The 9/11 guys didn't ask for anything. They just killed people, destroyed an American icon, panicked Dubya and his cronies into an idiot reaction. But they didn't fly into the twin towers waving a piece of paper with an agenda on it.'

'You haven't killed anyone,' said Tudor evenly, 'or destroyed anything. You're not suicide bombers. Even your guns are fake.'

'We've taken the ship,' she said, 'we can do what we like. If we want to kill people, we'll kill people. If we want to blow things up, we'll do that too.'

'You don't understand, do you?' Tudor wasn't bluffing. He didn't think she did.

'Understand what?'

'That the way Western democracies work is by appearing as unlike dictatorships as possible. In a dictatorship authority is always visible. Dictatorships rule on the basis of fear and coercion whereas democracies operate by consent. Dictators use iron fists; elected leaders hide them in velvet gloves. That doesn't mean they're not there.'

'I really don't need a lesson in political theory,' she said, disdainfully, 'Particularly one for twelve year olds.'

'Well excuse me but I think you do,' said Tudor, condescendingly. 'You seem to think that you and your friends have won something, that you've proved a point. That's not the case.'

'We control the ship,' she said. 'I want you as a mouthpiece. You're hostage number one and you'll come to no harm provided you do as you're told.'

She was blustering. Tudor told her so, angrily now.

'It's like the Falklands,' he said. 'Britain as a mature democracy had a relaxed attitude to the islands and didn't maintain a serious military garrison. That seemed to make them vulnerable to a rapacious dictatorship. So the Argentinians did what you've done. They took the islands and they were able to do so because they were not obviously defended. They were part of the free world and we treated them like that. However the Argentine

Government were hopelessly naïve and in due course, and with a distressing and unnecessary loss of life, they were expelled and the government of General Galtieri was overthrown. It's the same here. The nature of the *Duchess* is that she appears vulnerable. In fact she has to appear vulnerable if she is to perform her essential function. No one wants to take a holiday on a floating fortress. However there are detailed and sophisticated plans for dealing with situations such as this and people like you.'

'Malvinas,' she said, 'they were the Malvinas. And that's a grotesque Enid Blyton version of what actually happened and it has nothing, absolutely nothing to do with what's happening here and now.'

She was still blustering.

He told her so, angry now, 'and if you don't listen to me you'll end up dead. Your friends, too. Any time now the Master-at-Arms will press the button, put the relevant plan into action and you lot will be finished.'

She smiled the truculent smile of the super-confident or the impossibly naïve. Both, actually, thought Tudor.

'We could throw you overboard right now,' she said. 'You don't seem to realize. We're in charge. We are the masters now. We control the ship.'

Tudor shrugged.

'If you say so,' he said. In a sense, he supposed, she was right. His Falklands analogy was actually quite accurate, but the period between the coup or invasion or hijack or whatever and the arrival of the cavalry was a dodgy one. His own position like that of the officers on the bridge was undeniably fraught. For the time being at least.

'So. All right. What do you want?'

She appeared to relax.

'That's more like it,' she said. 'We'll make a little video. You'll have a list of our demands to read out but you'll frame it with a sympathetic and expert explanation of what's going on and why we're right.'

'And what *are* your demands?' he asked.

She smiled, apparently feeling that she'd regained an initiative. 'That's for me to decide and for you to find out. So are you going to co-operate?'

'I don't seem to have any alternative,' he said. 'But I wish you'd listen to what I have to say.'

'There'll be plenty of time for that,' she said. 'You and I are going to be spending quite a time with each other. I shall be interested in hearing some of your theories. And you may learn a thing or two by seeing what terrorism and hijacking are like in real life.'

Somewhere out on the crepuscular bridge a phone rang. After a few shrill tintinnabulations they ceased and an Irish voice spoke in surly monosyllables. Then a combat-geared figure appeared in the doorway.

'It's the girl,' said the goon. 'She wants to speak to the professor.'

Tipperary Tatler considered the request for a moment, then shrugged and said, 'I don't see why not. Give him the phone.'

Which he did. The woman's acquiescence seemed, to Tudor, further evidence of amateurism. In a similar situation he wouldn't have let himself talk to anyone except under strict supervision.

'Tell her,' said the Irish leaderene, 'that we'll be sending down a video shortly.'

'I'm to tell you that they'll be sending down a video.'

'Oh.' Elizabeth Burney sounded pertly amused.

'And we expect to see it broadcast on the ship's closed circuit TV within the half-hour,' said Tudor's captor, and he duly and obediently repeated the expectation, which was greeted with a sharp disbelieving laugh.

'I'm with the Master-at-arms,' said Elizabeth. 'He's an ex-SAS major with a karate platinum belt and a very old-fashioned moustache. He seems unnervingly anxious to kill people. Dishy but disturbing. I think you should warn your new friends that they have real trouble pending. Meanwhile there's just one thing he needs to know.'

'I'll pass the message on,' said Tudor.

'The major wants to know if they're armed.'

'Absolutely not,' he said. 'I'm fine. And being treated very nicely thank you.'

The goon and the girl looked at him, irritated, as if they were having second thoughts about allowing this conversation, as well they might.

'Just tell your friend that we'll be sending out the video shortly and meanwhile not to do anything stupid. And that goes for everyone else on board.'

Tudor smiled. 'I'm to tell you not to do anything stupid and that goes for everyone else on board,' he parroted.

'I'm sure Major Timbers will be trembling at the knees,' she said. 'Meanwhile we'll look forward to the film show. Take care. Over and out.'

There was a click, a buzz of static, then a dialling tone.

He handed the set back.

'Right,' he said, 'if we have a film to make I think I ought to have a look at the script.'

'I'm glad you're seeing sense,' she said.

'Sense is emphatically not what I'm seeing,' he said. 'Far from it. I've told you that I think you've got yourself in to a mess and it's going to become more of a mess and much much worse for you the longer you persevere with this silly charade. My playing along with what you want doesn't imply surrender or acquiescence or anything at all except, well . . . 'playing along with you'. I'll do just that but it doesn't mean you're out of trouble.'

She smirked in a way that seemed mildly deranged, then took a piece of paper from some hidden fold in her garment and handed it to Tudor.

'Demands,' she said. 'I'd like you to read them to camera but I don't want it to look as if you're being coerced in any way. So no script. Just a few cue-words and phrases. The whole thing should look like a nice cosy interview on daytime 'Judy'. Definitely Richard and Judy rather than Paxman or Humphries. Think David Frost. It's a conversation not an interrogation.'

'Anything you say,' he said, frowning over the green child-like handwriting. 'George Bush and Tony Blair to apologize profusely and in person at United Nations for invasion of Iraq. President Putin to withdraw all Russian troops from Chechnya.' He glanced up. 'You don't think perhaps you're being just a tiny bit optimistic?' he asked. She looked back just as scornfully and he glanced down again. 'Religious schools to be abolished,' he read. 'Hunting with hounds to be universally outlawed.'

'Are you going to make eating meat an offence?' he asked, not altogether good-naturedly.

She scowled.

'I know you think we're being naïve,' she said, 'but the fact is that most people around the world agree with us. But they're too oppressed and frightened to say so.'

Tudor nodded, all too aware that the way he did it made the gesture seem patronizing.

'Just let me rough out some notes,' he said, yawning. He suddenly felt extraordinarily tired, light-headed even. A combination of age and stress, he supposed.

Seconds later he realized he was passing out.

Only a nano-second later, he actually did so.

9

He felt as if he were coming out from under an anaesthetic. His throat was dry and sore at the back. His chest ached and his vision was blurred. He was aware of concerned, smiling, female, almost beatific faces looking down on him and wishing him well. The feeling was impotent but agreeable.

'Er . . . ' he said.

'No need to say anything,' said an Australian voice which he recognized as Elizabeth Burney's. 'You've been through a little bit of an ordeal. Done well. We're all impressed. Even me.'

He tried to speak again and failed once more.

'Don't worry,' she said, 'Major Timbers says it usually takes about twenty minutes to get your voice back. After that you'll be talking quite normally. So I've got a magical little window of opportunity into which I can get a word. A rare treat.' She giggled. Tudor had an uneasy feeling that her head had been turned by the galloping major with the moustache and exotic belt.

'So sshhh!,' She put a finger to her mouth.

'You've been gassed as I imagine you know. Rupert won't be too specific about it. Just describes it as 'standard-issue kit' — whatever that means.'

Rupert eh? So the major had a first name already.

'He's the Master-at-Arms,' she said, wide-eyed, 'but I expect you knew that. Most people on board call him 'the Jaunty' or 'the Jonty'. You learn something new every day. Every ship has one. Well, every ship except Filipino rust-buckets or Taiwanese fishing smacks. Our friends, the Irish, never had a prayer against a top-class Jonty with a crack team. Major Rupert has a crack team. They double up as everything you can imagine. One of the gentleman hosts is a genius with a jemmy; his explosives expert is a drummer in the jazz band; two of the wine-waiters are snipers with medals from Bisley. You wouldn't want to mess with them even if you were serious al-Qaeda suicide-squaddies. And these guys certainly aren't.'

She smiled encouragingly.

'They're in the brig. They'll be interrogated properly. Rupert supervises that with the two ballroom dancing instructors. He does nasty and the wife does nice. It's all rather wonderful.'

He wanted to ask more about the gas and

she seemed to guess as much.

'Rupert's keeping pretty shtumm about some aspects of the operation,' she said. 'He won't say exactly what the gas was and he won't say how it was introduced. He was actually rather keen to storm the bridge with stun-grenades and stuff. He seemed a bit depressed that we all wanted something stealthier and unmessy. He said storming the bridge would be good training for his 'boys' but I think the real reason was that he wanted to hurt someone, maybe kill them. I get the impression that, provided it can be justified, he's slightly into killing people. Anyway whatever sent you all to beddy-byes was presumably pumped in through the air-conditioning or maybe the sprinkler system.'

The other smiling female mopped Tudor's brow with some sort of dampish cloth. It smelt of disinfectant and cheap scent, like the sort of face-towel flight attendants give out on airlines. He seemed to be back in his cabin rather than the ship's sick-bay.

'We retrieved the list of demands which was babyish, frankly, but I dare say you found time to read it before the gas hit.'

She sighed.

'We'll leave you now,' she said. 'Try and get some sleep. I'll come back in an hour or so. You may have forgotten but it's Sunday. I thought we might go to church service. They're doing matins at eleven which is just over an hour's time. You can say thank you to God for your safe deliverance.'

The girls left. Their absence rendered him oddly deflated.

He couldn't sleep so stayed supine, staring at the ceiling and thought. He was alive but could easily have been dead. At least he thought he was alive. Limbo or purgatory, if not heaven or hell, could perfectly well have been a cabin on the *Duchess* being ministered to by a couple of pretty girls. On balance, however, he was reasonably convinced that he was alive and moderately well on the high seas. He had, though, behaved recklessly and must try not to do so again. Had the Irish hijackers been even moderately professional he would almost certainly not have been spared. On the other hand he had got away with it and would, with reasonable luck, be regarded as some sort of hero. Cool in a crisis and an expert at this sort of thing; not just an armchair expert. In any event he would certainly have put one over on Sir Goronwy Watkyn. Not to mention Chief Inspector Emeritus Freddy Grim.

But what on earth had that gang been playing at? It was almost as if they were students pulling off a stunt during rag week.

He wondered what would happen now. The ship was beyond territorial waters and therefore beyond any one country's jurisdiction. International law of the sea would apply although this was, he confessed to himself, not one of his major areas of expertise. Maritime Law he knew was based on the Laws of Oleron which had been codified by Eleanor of Aquitaine. In the event of mutiny on board a Royal Naval ship the mutineers were tried by courts martial and if found guilty hanged from the yard arm in front of the assembled crew. This was what happened to the guilty *Bounty* men. At the Spithead Mutiny of 1797 it was judged that their demands were legitimate, therefore no one was strung up. At the Mutiny of the Nore which followed shortly it was judged that the legitimate demands had all been satisfied after Spithead so the ring-leaders were executed, as was traditional when every man-jack took part of the insurrection and mass execution of all hands would have been impractical.

On merchant ships mutineers were tried by civil courts. However, if he were honest he couldn't be certain what was done to passengers who rose up against the ship's legitimate authority. It wasn't a frequent occurrence. Bearing in mind the so-called war on terrorism which had been carried on since the destruction of the New York World Trade Centre on 9/11 anyone attempting to hijack a cruise-ship could reasonably expect to be shot out of hand. The US Marine Corps didn't take prisoners.

He sighed.

It was all quite mystifying. And the 'demands' had been grotesquely naïve. It was almost as if the gang had gone into operation demanding the answer no, determined to fail. But what would be the point of that? Perhaps they had been hired by Riviera so that the shipping line could be made to look good. There was a horrid plausibility about that in the modern world. On the other hand the ragtag band of brothers and sisters he had encountered on the bridge didn't feel like actors from Central Casting. Tudor was not, by nature, a conspiracy theorist belonging firmly in the cock-up camp. He found it inconceivable that even in the age of spin a cruise company would stage an act of high-seas piracy in order to demonstrate the reliability of their own security procedures and systems.

This afternoon he was scheduled to deliver his 'Mutiny on the *Bounty*' talk. This seemed at one and the same time both more and yet less significant. The incident this morning gave him first-hand experiences on which to draw and yet a contemporary brush with disaster made a history lecture seem pretty irrelevant. Why care about mid-Pacific mid-eighteenth century when you'd experienced a state-of-the-art, man-of-the-moment equivalent in the here-and-now? Tudor would have his work cut out to demonstrate the reason for talking about the *Bounty* when what everyone wanted to know about was the *Duchess*. Heigh-ho!

He dozed. Images flickered across his subconscious like scenes from an old movie. He saw lifeboats from *Titanic* overturning; Trevor Howard as Captain Bligh berating Marlon Brando as Fletcher Christian — were they actually in the same movie?; Jack Hawkins in *The Cruel Sea*; Humphrey Bogart as Captain Queeg rolling dice in the Herman Wouk classic whose name eluded him. *The Caine Mutiny* that was it. Mutiny seemed the operative word and yet what had happened this morning was not a mutiny in the accepted sense.

His mind was wandering. Bloody nerve gas. Bound to have a disorientating effect. Wouldn't be a nerve gas if it didn't. It would wear off presumably. Timbers and Co must be aware of its properties. He'd be right as rain in a minute or so. Church parade would sort him out. Hand of God and all that. Thinking of Timbers and his lot though gave one pause for thought, didn't it? It was obviously essential in the post-9/11, Iraq-invasion world for ships such as the *Duchess* to carry discreet private armies as protection against terrorism in any shape or form, but private armies were, almost by definition, susceptible to bribes and blandishments. That was, after all, the definition of a mercenary.

What God abandoned, these defended,
And saved the sum of things for pay.

Housman. It was a cynical trade. You made yourself available to the highest bidder. Patriotism, loyalty, belief, fanaticism, call it what you like . . . these buttered no parsnips with men like Major Timbers. Both the Umlauts and the Prince of Araby could match any bids made by, well, anyone. On the other hand, Tudor guessed, selling out to the highest bidder would, if it meant changing sides in mid-stream, be ultimately bad for business. Trust might be too cosy a word for terrorism and its counterpart, but there would have to be honour among thieves. If you got a reputation for breaking contracts you wouldn't last long even in that murky world.

He must have dozed off again for when he was next aware of anything it was of a hand on his shoulder and the radiant and intelligent eyes of Elizabeth Burney staring into his.

'Church parade,' she said, half-mocking, half-affectionate, not even marginally respectful. 'If you're not feeling a whole lot better already you will be after a hymn or two and some robust words from our glorious captain. I had a quick look at the menu and they're doing 'Eternal Father Strong to Save'; the Old Testament lesson is Genesis Seven.'

'There went in two and two unto Noah into the ark . . . the male and the female,' intoned Tudor wearily. 'That's a bit corny.'

'Attaboy,' said Elizabeth clapping her hands together. 'No permanent ill-effects from nerve gas. Just like Shiver-my-Timbers said.'

'Shiver-my?' repeated Tudor.

'Someone called Major Timbers simply has to have a nickname,' she said. 'And I don't, under the circumstances, see how it could conceivably be anything else.'

'And I suppose the second lesson is Matthew, Chapter Twenty-four, verse Thirty-eight.

''For as in the days that were before the flood they were eating and drinking, marrying and giving in marriage, until the day that Noah entered into the ark, and knew not until the flood came and took them all away.' '

'How did you know that?' asked the girl, impressed.

'They always do a double-Noah on the first Sunday after embarcation,' he said. 'It's a bit obvious, but passengers seem to like it. The idea of being descended in some curious way from Mr and Mrs Noah rather appeals to them though I don't think the ark would have satisfied modern safety regs and I don't suppose the catering would have been any great shakes.'

'No rum punch in the captain's bar,' said Elizabeth. 'I always imagine the ark must have been incredibly smelly.'

'Probably,' said Tudor. He was beginning to feel a lot better. Heroic even. He stood up and went into the bathroom where he splashed his face liberally with cold water.

'Five minutes before kick off,' she said, chirpily, opening the cabin door and hustling him outside.

They walked briskly and in silence along the corridors and up to the doors of the cinema which doubled up, on these occasions, as morning chapel, ecumenical. It was slightly unconvincing, tasteless even, but not as unconvincing or even, in a manner of speaking, tasteless as the figure standing at the entrance clutching a Bible and prayer book and wearing a cassock and a sanctimonious expression.

It was Freddie Grim, but to Tudor's amazement, no longer retired Detective Chief Inspector Grim, but the Reverend Grim. Policeman Fred appeared to have taken to Holy Orders.

10

Grim's was a bizarre sermon. ' 'Water, water everywhere and not a drop to drink',' he began, in a nasal sing-song voice which reminded Tudor of Jonathan Miller's vicar in 'Beyond the Fringe.' ' 'My brother Esau is an hairy man, but I am a smooth man'.' Grim's words made about as much sense. His theme was H_2O but he was drowned by it, engulfed. No ark for Grim.

In a perverse way Tudor quite enjoyed trying to work out what exactly it was that the newly ordained preacher was trying to say. He was certainly moving in a mysterious way but it was difficult if not impossible to work out what lay behind the mystery and if there was any method at all in the apparent madness. Tudor wouldn't have given him a licence.

Meanwhile the *Duchess* was heading into a storm. The curtain behind the makeshift altar was waving mesmerizingly and metronomically at the beginning of the service but by the time they reached the second hymn it had moved from the gentle sleepy seduction of Force Five to the dangerous billowing of Eight or Nine. Preacher Grim had to brace his sea legs and hold fast to the lectern. One or two of the congregation wove an uneasy path out of the cinema.

'The animals went in two by two,' said Reverend Grim. 'Two by two. Not individually one by one; not even in threesomes where one of them would have been what later generations call a gooseberry; not in a herd, nor a flock, nor a crowd, nor a group, nor a team, but two by two.'

Here he paused and glared round the auditorium as the curtain flapped behind him and the floor rose and fell.

'Two by two,' he repeated, 'two by two.'

'The animals are going out two by two,' whispered Elizabeth behind her hand as another queasy couple made for the exit.

Grim now seemed lost for words, his attention distracted by the gathering storm and the diminishing congregation. Then, with an obvious effort, he pulled himself together and relaunched himself. 'When,' he said, 'in a previous life I was often confronted by sin and its wages I found myself deliberating on the subject long and hard. Long and hard.' And here, he stared around the cinema with the demonic gaze of an Old Testament prophet or a Methodist preacher in the Wesleyan tradition.

'Why's he repeating everything?' asked

Elizabeth in another whisper.

'Because he can't think what to say next,' said Tudor unkindly. 'Or,' he added even less kindly, 'because it's something they taught him in preaching college. Trick of the trade.'

'What I learned in a life surrounded by criminals and immersed in crime was that actually the most serious crime of all, that of murder, the taking of human life, which is not only a crime against humanity but a sin against God, murder is very rarely a criminal crime. That is to say that in my experience — in my very varied and lengthy experience — I very rarely came across criminals who killed.

'Murder was much more frequently . . . very much more frequently . . . committed by those who, like the animals who went into the ark, lived their lives two by two. For as the wife said of her husband, or it could just as well have been the husband saying of the wife, when asked, if during their long marriage, he, or she, had ever considered divorce, replied, 'Divorce never, murder frequently.' He stared at the now thin congregation, eyes revolving unnervingly and was rewarded with a mild titter.

'Lady Longford,' said Tudor under his breath, 'speaking of the noble Earl.'

'It's a very old joke,' whispered Elizabeth, 'and almost certainly apocryphal.'

God alone knew where Freddie Grim went from here. He seemed to be talking about the perils yet sanctity of marriage and to be pegging his remarks to the notion that many of those cruising aboard the Good Ship *Duchess* were celebrating significant wedding anniversaries. For couples such as this read animals two by two; for the *Duchess* read the ark; and presumably for Noah read the Master of the *Duchess*, Sam Hardy.

It was odd, thought Tudor, that the Master was not present. Perhaps, aware of the impending storm, he had decided that his place was on the bridge. Yet that seemed unlikely for Sam Hardy only ever thought of the bridge as the place to be when he was showing passengers around it. He would normally be here with a big black prayer book leading matins the way ship captains were popularly supposed to.

'So you see,' said the preacher, 'nothing could seem cosier or more companionable, or safer than a voyage at sea in the company of one's beloved partner. The ark represented sanctuary and safety. She was a refuge from a naughty world. Indeed in that particularly disastrous moment in the world's history she represented the only place in which one could live. Everybody else perished.

'And yet' — and here he wagged a finger at

his now seriously depleted audience — 'and yet, the safety of the closed room which is another way of looking at a modern cruise liner or an ancient ark is a deception and a delusion. There is no safety at sea, no safety in an enclosed space but, above all, my brothers and sisters there is no safety with those you consider your nearest and dearest. It was Jean Paul Sartre, no Christian he, who told us that hell is other people. *Huis Clos.*'

He paused and gazed round again. Tudor had a distinct impression that either he or the preacher were going mad. 'It was right for Noah,' said Grim. 'Noah was six hundred years old when he built the Ark and when he disembarked he lived on for another three hundred and fifty. And it was all right for those who sailed with him. But it wasn't all right for those that were left behind. Remember what happened? 'Every living substance was destroyed which was upon the face of the ground, both man and cattle, and the creeping things, and the fowl of the heaven, and they were destroyed from the earth: and Noah only remained alive, and they that were with him in the ark'.'

'What's he trying to say?' muttered Elizabeth.

'I think he's telling us that he knows his

Bible inside out,' said Tudor, 'otherwise I just don't get it.'

'So what, in the end, did God mean by this?' asked Grim. 'What is the underlying message in the story of Noah and the ark and the animals that went in two by two and all those creeping things and the clean and the unclean? What possible relevance can it have for the rest of us?'

And now he looked around with a baleful air of triumph as if he had come to the end of a difficult task but had prevailed in the end.

'Our Master on board this ship will not live to be nine hundred and fifty years old as Noah did,' he said. 'But at the same time we would do well to ponder the words with which our Lord ended the dreadful story of the flooding of the earth and the saving of the human race on board ship. He said, 'I will not again curse the ground any more for man's sake; for the imagination of man's heart is evil from his youth; neither will I again smite any more every thing living, as I have done'.'

And here the retired policeman smiled a huge grin of baleful self-satisfaction, crossed himself and said, 'And so in the name of God the Father, God the Son and God the Holy Ghost, Amen.' After which in a voice subtly changed from that of inspirational preacher to official factotum, he announced that the final hymn was to be 'Eternal Father strong to save whose hand hath bound the restless wave' and during it a collection would be taken in aid of the Royal National Lifeboat Association.

Tudor sang lustily and gave generously; Elizabeth remained stumm and gave nothing. At the end of the hymn they all bowed their heads while Grim pronounced a blessing and told them to go in peace. This they duly did.

'Fascinating sermon,' said Tudor, outside in the lobby. 'Fascinating' was one of the most useful words in his semantic armoury, suggesting huge enthusiasm while actually doing no such thing. He suspected, from Grim's sickly grin of acknowledgement that the policeman/priest recognized the device for what it was.

'I'm glad you enjoyed it,' she said.

It was on the tip of Tudor's tongue to point out that he hadn't broached the matter of enjoyment, but instead he said, guardedly, 'Plenty of food for thought.'

'Drink for thought,' said Elizabeth accurately but unhelpfully. 'One of the most liquid addresses I've ever heard.'

Grim turned his rheumy eyes on her as if noticing her for the first time.

'Thank you my dear,' he said, clearly not meaning it.

He then reverted to Tudor and said,

'Certain amount of excitement this morning, I understand.'

It was a question masquerading as a statement.

' 'Exciting' is a bit strong,' said Tudor wearily and warily. 'All in a day's work for people such as you and I. There was an incident of sorts but it was all easily resolved. No harm done. A handful of silly people handcuffed together in the brig but nothing that couldn't be resolved by a mixture of intellectual rigour and a straight bat.'

'How very British,' said Grim. 'I look forward to hearing more in due course.'

Saying which he turned to other members of the congregation who were still filtering out into the Sunday morning.

'I fancy a walk round the deck,' he said to Elizabeth Burney. 'Coming?'

She said she thought that sounded like a half decent idea and would probably do him good so they went up a flight of stairs to the promenade deck, shoved open one of the heavy doors and were beaten back by the wind which was rising in strength.

'OK?' asked Tudor.

'Yup,' she said, looking frail and vulnerable but no longer fooling her mentor.

They leaned into the wind and walked.

Seconds later they bumped into Mandy

Goldslinger. She was wearing a designer track-suit and walking in the wrong direction.

'*Dottore!*' she screeched above the gathering storm. 'You're dead. It's official. How's it feel?'

She was clutching a piece of paper. It turned out to be the hard copy of an e-mail from the obituaries department of the *Daily Telegraph* in London. The author was David Twiston-Davies, the paper's chief obituarist and he was researching a eulogy of the distinguished Criminal Student Dr Tudor Cornwall who, he was reliably informed, had just perished at sea under distressing and violent circumstances.

'Good, eh?' cackled La Goldslinger mirthlessly. 'Never believe anything you read in the newspapers. Had you on the right ship though. Or off it, eh!' and she shoved him in the shoulder almost knocking him over.

'Ah,' said Tudor, making the obvious connection with the sinister amateurs with whom he had been grappling earlier in the day. 'Not *Tipperary*?'

'I thought that might interest you,' she said. 'You might want to run it past the prisoners in the bilges. But that's not all.'

A larger than usual wave rocked the boat causing all three to stagger and clutch on to the nearest railings. The next revelation from Mandy Goldslinger also made Tudor and Elizabeth stagger though not as literally as the wave.

'I called Twiston-Davies,' she said, 'to tell him that you were still very much alive. He sounded halfway between relieved and irritated. Said he'd put a lot of work in on the piece and was I quite sure as they were rather hoping to make you their lead — it being a slow death day. He also said his informant was absolutely adamant about your having passed away. He was an old friend of yours as well, apparently. The Visiting Professor at the IISWP.'

'Don't tell me,' said Tudor, 'I think I can guess.'

But Elizabeth Burney did the guesswork for him.

'Ashley Carpenter,' she said. 'It has to be Ashley.'

Ms Goldslinger arched immaculately painted eyebrows and glanced from one to the other.

'How did you know?' she asked.

Tudor and Elizabeth glanced at each other and shrugged.

'He had to crop up sooner or later,' said Tudor.

Elizabeth simply frowned.

'Greatly exaggerated,' he said, 'rumours of my death.'

''Course you're not dead, darling,' said the cruise director. 'I know a stiff when I see one. Had enough in my day. Hardly a cruise goes by when a gentleman host or his client doesn't topple off the perch and end up in the refrigerator between the lobster and the Aberdeen Angus rib-eye.'

Elizabeth Burney looked incredulous and seemed on the verge of speech but Tudor quelled her with a vividly alive-looking glare.

'So the Twister thinks I'm dead,' he said. 'How so? Who's his source?'

'Well,' said Mandy with a lascivious leer, 'the story seems to have come out of the International Institute for the Study of World Republicanism.'

'Which must be somewhere in North Carolina,' said Tudor.

'Or Bulgaria,' said Elizabeth.

'Close but no cigar,' said Mandy. 'You're on track. It's not really international, it doesn't really study anything, it . . . oh well, shit, it's a Mickey Mouse sort of a place but they seem to have stacks of money and nothing much to do but make trouble and stuff.'

The stormy winds did blow and the trio braced their legs as the Arabian wives marched past in close formation and billowing burnooses, eyes firmly straight ahead and undeviating.

'So the International Institute for the Study of World Republicanism told the *Daily Telegraph* I was dead. Where are they when they are at home if not Bulgaria or North Carolina? Don't tell me. Bolivia. They're big in La Paz.'

''Fraid not,' said the cruise director. 'Irish outfit. The postal address is Limerick.'

11

Ashley Carpenter was Moriarty to Tudor's Sherlock Holmes.

It wasn't as simple as that. How could it be? Fact was, in his experience, always more complicated and far-fetched than fiction. He and Carpenter had an edgy, complex reality that the melodramatic Victorian cut-outs of Holmes and Moriarty necessarily lacked.

Carpenter had been satisfactorily absent from Tudor's life for a while now, to such an extent that Tudor almost believed he had vanished for good, perished in some unobserved disaster at his own Reichenbach Falls perhaps, or vanished into Mexican gunsmoke like Ambrose Bierce. Yet so far, Ashley had never quite gone away, and he always cropped up unexpectedly just when Tudor had almost forgotten him.

Not that he could ever entirely forget, not as long as the precocious Elizabeth Burney remained under his wing. Elizabeth was Carpenter's legacy, a farewell gift after that Visiting-Fellowship which made Tudor wince whenever he thought of it.

The two of them had been best of friends

at university — or so Tudor believed. Only years later when Ashley invited his former fellow-student to spend a semester in his hometown 'uni' did Tudor come to believe otherwise. Ashley had asked him down under and then done a bunk and set Tudor up on a murder rap. It sort of hadn't worked out and in some curious and still unexplained act of final revenge Carpenter had bequeathed him Elizabeth, his own former mistress. Or so Tudor believed. It was not something he and Elizabeth ever discussed. Indeed until now the words Ashley Carpenter had scarcely passed their lips. Theirs was an unusual relationship, founded largely on evasion and unspoken words.

They had in the phrase of the day, 'moved on.' In another piece of bromide vernacular they had drawn a line under what had gone before. And yet as they both knew neither option was really available. Life and lives were not like that. They were all of a piece. You could not simply create a new identity for yourself and repudiate all that had gone before. Your past was part of your present and would inevitably inform your future. And Ashley Carpenter was part of Tudor's past and Elizabeth's as well. Try as they might they could not eradicate him and pretend he had never been. Now here he was, back with a vengeance.

'So,' said Tudor, as the ship tossed and they turned back down the starboard promenade deck, buffeted by the galeforce wind, 'did you know anything about this?'

'Of course not.' The girl looked put out. 'Ashley's history.' she said. 'You know that.'

Cornwall leaned against the rail and looked out over the swirling whitecaps, feeling the salt on his face. 'Maybe you're Ashley's sleeper. You've been put in place, lulled me into a false sense of well-being and acceptance and then just when I least expect it you explode. An emotional suicide bomber, programmed to go off at the most lethal moment.'

She snorted. 'Clever analogy,' she said, 'but insulting. I'm shocked. Anyone would think you didn't trust me.'

'Let's go in,' he said abruptly. 'I need a strong coffee and a straight think.'

It was a relief to escape the raw wind and spume and to find oneself rocking comparatively gently at the bar while Boris's espresso machine fizzed and fumed.

'Did you like Ashley?' he asked the girl.

She wrinkled her nose. 'That's sort of the wrong question,' she said thoughtfully. 'Liking or not liking was never part of the equation with Ashley. He was a sort of Svengali figure and I was mesmerized. You don't like or dislike people in situations like that. I was in thrall. *Thrall*. There's a word. I'm not even exactly sure what it means but that's what I was in. Bad place to be. Much better off out of it.'

Their coffees came. The ship rocked.

'Maybe I was in thrall to Ashley once upon a time too,' said Tudor. He felt comfortable suddenly. The insecurity of the abortive hijacking and the threat of the storm outside seemed to have abated. Disconcertingly he found himself thinking of modern ship-wrecks. *Titanic*, of course, but more recently the car ferry *Estonia* which capsized in the Baltic in 1994 killing more than 800. Tudor's own opinion regarding the disaster was that it was an accident brought about by faulty design, shoddy maintenance — greed, indiscipline and a furious storm. There was however, a conspiracy theory lcd by a former TV reporter called Jutta Rabe. Tudor had read her book and talked to many of those concerned. Jutta Rabe had made a film of the tragedy starring Greta Scacchi as an intrepid German TV reporter. Tudor had thought it ridiculous. However he could not completely discount the theory that the ship's bows had been blown off by explosive charges planted by former KGB agents who escaped in a lifeboat and were never found. The notion seemed fanciful and melodramatic, but then conspiracy theories nearly always did and sometimes they were correct.

More to the point, in a way, was the sense of complete security which preceded the capsize. Hundreds of people were drinking in the bars; many others were in their cabins, tucked up, asleep, lulled there by the seductively soporific motion of the ship. Much as now, moving to and fro on a bar stool, contemplating a serious double espresso in five star comfort alongside a pretty person with dangerous legs and lips. What could be safer?

It reminded him of that remark in Conan Doyle about the smiling English countryside actually being a much more dangerous place than the snarling English city. Boris' Bar on the *Duchess* had an almost womb-like quality with its serried ranks of single malts and insect-riddled tequilas. Boris himself shimmered about shaking cocktails smoothly and exuding a reassuring charm. The carpets were thick. The sepia prints of ancient ships and seafarers spoke of history and tried and tested values. There was a scent of expensive cigar and Chanel.

Yet . . . it would be stretching a point to say that they were sitting in a floating death-trap but this place was nowhere as safe as it seemed. Like life itself. One of the obvious discoveries he had made in the course of his academic career was that the only way most people got through life was because they believed that life would always continue in a placid almost somnolent almost entirely predictable fashion. If you could see the horrors around the corner you'd give up immediately, slash your wrists or throw yourself somewhere from a great height.

This was an obvious fact but academics devoted their lives to stating the obvious in a mildly obfuscatory manner designed to impress the laity. It was almost a definition of his role: to spend a long time and much research in order to demonstrate a proposition which most people thought too obvious to be worth discussing. You took some corny old adage such as 'Pride comes before a fall' and conducted a number of case-studies, got a market research company to issue question-naires to demonstrate that in 51 per cent of all known cases pride did indeed come before a fall, but that notwithstanding this, the chances of it doing so were significantly greater if you were a low earning smoker from the Scottish borders than if you were an affluent retired non-smoker in the Home Counties.

The proposition he now considered was how the time to really worry about some unexpected disaster was when you were feeling most secure. That was when these things struck. That was what happened on the *Estonia* and the *Titanic*. Those on board, believed, against all the evidence that the vessels were unsinkable. 'Blow, blow thou winter wind/ Thou art not so unkind/ As man's ingratitude.' Shakespeare. *As you Like it*. But had Shakespeare ever really been in a tempest? Were his storms truly convincing? Did he, like J.M.W. Turner, lash himself to the mast of a struggling ship in order to experience the reality of a storm at sea. Did it really matter? What price imagination?

'Penny for them,' said Elizabeth, at his elbow.

'I was just thinking how good the coffee was and how much I needed it. Also that I'm speaking this afternoon and I'm not sure how much enthusiasm I can really muster for the *Bounty* and Bligh.'

'I don't believe a word of it,' she said. 'You were thinking about Ashley. Trying to get inside his head.'

'Why ask if you know the answers?' he said, 'Little Miss Know All.'

She was right of course. If she had been wrong he wouldn't have been so unreasonably irritated. Getting inside the head of your opponent, the criminal, was one of the first essentials of good detection. It was the most obvious reason for the West's inability to cope with al-Qaeda. Very few westerners, especially those in the security services, had the knowledge and sophistication to get inside the heads of Islamic preachers or disaffected Asian youths. He, Tudor, probably didn't have what it took to get inside the head of Ashley Carpenter. Nevertheless he knew that that was where the answers lay. Psychological understanding.

It was why the old-fashioned custom whereby coppers hung out with villains, drank in their dens, flirted with their molls and were, shamefully, often as bent as the criminals they were supposed to be chasing, was in some ways more effective than the modern ivory tower methods involving DNA and the internet. Same went for crime reporting. The old-fashioned ways may have seemed primitive or politically incorrect but they were often effective.

'You're away with the fairies,' she said. The ship lurched suddenly and their coffee cups slid in unison down the bar counter spilling as they went.

'I suppose,' he admitted. Then, in self-vindication, said, 'I was only thinking. There's a lot to think about.'

'Fancy sharing some of them?'

He looked at her, wondering, not for the first time, what was going on inside that pretty little head of hers and then cursing himself for being so patronizing even though he was keeping these male-chauvinist thoughts to himself.

'The more I know about crime,' he said, 'the more I understand how little I know. That's life, but even so. I mean, I think Ashley is obsessional about me for some reason I don't properly understand. I always liked him. Or thought I did. He seems to hate me. I don't understand why. And if I don't fully understand why I'll never be able to predict what he'll do next. Which is true of nearly all criminal activity.'

'Ashley is beyond understanding,' she said, with feeling. 'He's almost certainly criminally insane which means that someone who is sane and law-abiding is in serious trouble when it comes to comprehending what makes Ashley tick. I don't think anyone who isn't barmy can ever properly come to terms with someone who is — despite what shrinks say. But, hey, I thought this cruise was supposed to be a rest?'

Tudor retrieved his coffee and sipped.

'That's the theory,' he said. 'Sometimes they are. Just as often they're so stressful you

120

need a holiday when you get home.'

He suddenly felt a need to unburden himself and slip into confessional mode. However, he was saved by the bell — literally. The bell was electronic and amplified and signified twelve noon. When it had finished sounding a voice came over the Tannoy. It was Scottish.

'Hi, ladies and gentlemen, boys and girls,' it began unpromisingly. 'This is your Staff Captain, Angus Donaldson, speaking from the bridge. It is twelve noon and we are approximately three hundred miles west of Ireland steaming at a speed of approximately fifteen knots through winds of around Force Seven. And the first thing I should say, apart from wishing all and every one of you a very good day, is to apologize on behalf of the Master of the *Duchess*, Captain Sam Hardy. Unfortunately, Captain Sam became unwell in the night and is suffering from laryngitis.

'I am happy to tell you that he is not actually suffering. Indeed he ate a hearty breakfast and he would be here with us talking to you today were it not for the fact that due to the illness from which he is suffering he has lost his voice completely.'

Captain Donaldson had clearly not lost his. One after another not particularly funny

Scottish jokes, followed each other in a staccato stand-upspeakery of one-liners. Interspersed among these there were one or two more or less pertinent facts about the ship's position and prospects. Donaldson did not, at any stage, allude to the dramatic incident involving the *Tipperary Tatler* girl and her friends. After about five minutes of wittering he signed off with an old chestnut about an Englishman, a Welshman and a Scotsman and what people wore under their kilts.

Tudor looked at his pupil and she gazed back at him.

'What do you make of that?' he asked. 'Old Captain Birds Eye seemed his usual implausible self last night.'

'That's what I thought,' she said.

'So?'

'Fishy,' she said, arching her eyebrows. 'Captain overboard perhaps? A bridge too far?'

Tudor frowned but said nothing.

12

They lunched off caviar in the Dowager's Diner and sat at a table next to Prince Abdullah. Tudor always lunched off caviar when guest-lecturing. It was an extravagance he could otherwise not afford and it was relatively slimming despite the soured cream and the blinis. The restaurant, despite its kitsch name, was extravagantly elegant and reserved for the use of those in suites or the most expensive staterooms. Tudor and Elizabeth Burney somehow just made the cut largely thanks to the good offices of Mandy Goldslinger. Only Sir Goronwy and Lady Watkyn of the other guest speakers were similarly honoured. Little Freddie Grim was a class or two below in the Baroness Brasserie and gentlemen hosts such as Ambrose Perry were way beneath the salt and, almost, the water-line in the Butler's Pantry.

The Prince ate mulligatawny soup, steak and kidney pudding, and jam roly poly. In between courses he smoked untipped Passing Cloud cigarettes. Tudor and Elizabeth watched out of the corners of their eyes with an almost awed fascination.

Eventually when all three were drinking coffee and the Prince was smoking yet another cigarette, he spoke.

'I do hope,' he said, in a nasal parody of an Oxford-BBC-Wodehousian accent, 'that my smoking does not cause offence.'

Tudor and Elizabeth, both of whom would have much preferred a non-smoking dining-room, shook their heads and murmured polite nothings.

Evidently encouraged by this the Prince unbent.

'Smoking at mealtimes is customary in my country,' he said, smiling. 'Just as it used to be in yours. However, the use of nicotine appears to have become unfashionable. In fact' — and here he leaned towards them in a conspiratorial way — 'in fact, I am sorry to say that as the result of pressure from certain non-smoking passengers, the owners of the *Duchess* went so far as to propose a shipboard ban on the practice. Happily they have now desisted.'

The Prince was clearly eager to impart a confidence so Tudor encouraged him to do so.

'What made them do that?' he asked innocently.

'Aha,' said the Prince, stubbing out a cigarette and immediately lighting another.

'Money. As you say it speaks louder than words.'

Neither Tudor nor the girl were sure how to respond to this truism so they said nothing. However they both smiled in an encouraging way designed to make the Prince confide further.

'Between you and I,' he said conspiratorially, 'it was that fellow Umlaut. He is not a good man, Herr Umlaut. Not one of us.'

Tudor was tempted to say '*Ach so!*' or 'Don't mention the war'. Instead he merely muttered something inane about some of his best friends being German. He didn't much like the look of the Umlauts either, but it had nothing to do with xenophobia. He just didn't like the look of them. It was as simple as that. Or as complex. The half-empty, half-full argument.

'In any event,' said the Prince, 'he was easily defeated. I simply told the shipping company that if the *Duchess* was declared a no-smoking zone I should like my money back. With interest. And as I have booked the two largest and most expensive suites for the best part of the next ten years this represented a substantial amount of spondulicks, at least as far as a not particularly well-managed medium-sized commercial company is concerned.

'My grandfather made a fortune trading

with river steamers on the Euphrates. He also built the world's largest yacht. You have probably heard of her. *The Ethel Selina* named after my grandmother who was English and came from Letchworth. My beloved Granny Ethel.' The Prince smiled and blew a blue smoke ring at the ceiling watching it wistfully as it dissolved above him.

'Owning your own yacht, however, is, as you would put it, a mug's game. Which is why I prefer to make my home aboard the *Duchess.*'

This was not an option available to either Tudor or Elizabeth but they nevertheless nodded in dutiful agreement as if they too were in the Forbes' Magazine top hundred richest people in the world list. Then for a moment the three of them contemplated the coincidence which had thrown them together in such weird incongruity. Tudor was about to break the gathering ice with a hastily put-together platitude when the ship's klaxon sounded.

It was the daily message from the bridge but, contrary to usual practice, it was not the captain.

Tudor took a sip of wine and frowned.

'The captain seemed in good voice yesterday evening,' he said.

'Stentorian,' agreed Elizabeth.

'Like the proverbial foghorn,' said Prince Abdullah as the staff captain chuntered on with longitudes, latitudes, gale warnings and ancient jokes.

None of the three could be bothered listening. It was perfectly obvious that they were sailing through stormy weather but that they were more or less on schedule. This was the Atlantic Ocean after all and the sturdy old *Duchess* was designed to cope with her. She might toss about a bit but she would emerge unscathed and on time. After all she had been doing so for the best part of thirty years.

'I sense some form of rodent assailing the nostrils,' said the Prince. Tudor wondered what sort of language school had taught him to maul the English tongue in such a peculiarly archaic manner. Actually it probably wasn't a language school but some sort of mad tutor hired through some hopeless rival of Gabbitas and Thring, the educational employment agency.

'The Master's vocal chords appeared to be functioning with their usual stentorian efficiency,' said the Prince. 'Would you care to join me in a sticky?'

Tudor and Elizabeth looked at each other warily. It had been a hard and unusual day so far and Tudor had a lecture to deliver. Even so, both felt that they were on the verge of an interesting break-through. They were not exactly making a new friend but they seemed on the verge of crashing a hitherto forbidding barrier. In an unexpectedly threatening little world they could use any ally they could find. It would be good to have Prince Abdullah on side, however precariously.

They settled for a Calvados apiece.

'You come here often?' asked Tudor, disingenuously, as the Staff Captain finally signed off with yet another ghastly joke.

The Prince sighed. It seemed to Tudor that the sigh was both weary and wary — a sign of fatigue and caution.

'I feel at home here,' he said, 'but perhaps not as at home as I once did.'

Tudor and Elizabeth hung on his words, smiling encouragingly, saying nothing.

'They tried to stop smoking,' said the Prince, 'until I persuaded them that it was an abuse of civil liberties. Dashed impertinence. Like this hand-washing rigmarole. I don't hold with it.'

Because of something called the Norovirus, previously known as the Norwalk Virus, passengers were required to go through a ritual hand cleansing when boarding the ship or entering any of the restaurants. All passengers were given a piece of paper which contained the admonition: *we would like to remind you that the simplest preventative measure you can take to help maintain our healthy environment is to wash your hands frequently and thoroughly with soap for at least twenty seconds and rinse them well under running water. We strongly recommend that you follow this procedure each time you use the toilet, after coughing or sneezing, and before eating, drinking or smoking. Avoid touching your mouth.*

'Bloody cheek,' said the Prince, blowing blue smoke at the ceiling. 'If I want to wash my hands before smoking I'll decide for myself, thank you. I haven't been spoken to like that since I was eight years old and that was by matron at my boarding prep.'

The Prince seemed angry.

'I have been sailing on the *Duchess* for many years and I would like to sail on the *Duchess* for many years to come,' he said. 'I have paid the company massive quantities of spondulicks, much of it on account and in advance. In return I expect service and deference. Part of which' — and here his voice went up an octave or so — 'involves having a captain who is capable of being on the bridge and speaking to the ship's passengers on a daily basis. Laryngitis, shlaryngitis, as my Jewish friends would say.

Nelson would never have succumbed to such a thing. Horatio would have remained on the bridge at all times and spoken with the voice of an Englishman.'

Tudor felt that the Prince was in danger of muddling his Horatios but he said nothing, just nodded sympathetically and sipped his apple brandy.

'I'm speaking this afternoon,' he said, feeling that it was probably time to change the subject and wondering how much alcohol the Prince had consumed and whether this might prove to be a problem. He had always understood that Islam, to which presumably the Prince subscribed, involved an abstinence from alcoholic beverages, but he had seen enough of a certain sort of privileged adherent of any number of supposedly puritan creeds to realize that there were always some who considered themselves to be above the law, even if that law was God's.

'Ah. Break a leg!' said the Prince unexpectedly. 'I make it a practice never to attend lectures but I shall catch a little of what you have to say on the closed circuit television in my stateroom. On what are you holding forth?'

'I'm doing the Mutiny on the *Bounty*,' said Tudor.

'How apposite,' said the Prince. 'Or

perhaps not. I trust that our gallant captain is faring better than Captain Bligh at the hands of Fletcher Christian and his fellow desperadoes even if his voice has escaped him. Do you have anything new to tell us?'

'Well . . . ' Tudor thought for a moment. 'Not new exactly but my interpretation differs fundamentally from the view that Bligh was some sort of tyrannical bully who got his just deserts.'

'Ah,' said the Prince, 'a revisionist view.'

'You could say so,' said Tudor.

'I'm not sure that I share your charitable view of ships' captains,' said the Prince. 'Certainly in modern times I believe that they should subscribe to the view that the passenger is always right. Particularly when the passenger is myself.'

Saying which he rose unsteadily to his feet, smiled over enthusiastically, waved a hand in farewell and made for the exit, banging in to one or two tables as he did so.

13

His talk went well. The *Bounty* was an obvious subject. Even if everyone hadn't seen one or other of the movies and got a fix on Charles Laughton or Marlon Brando they still had a good idea of the basic story. Tudor was a Bligh man, believing that the captain of the ship was a maligned figure and a great seaman and that Fletcher Christian was unfairly romanticized. He had a good academic grasp of the subject and had even, once, visited Pitcairn Island and talked to the descendants of Fletcher Christian and his accomplices. On this occasion, however, he didn't think it appropriate to be too academically rigorous. The sort of audience you got in the ballroom of the *Duchess* was unlikely to want anything too demanding, especially after lunch.

What went down well, as always, with a cruise-ship audience was to try to evoke a picture of the ship as an island entire unto itself, a little self-contained community far from the reach of outside civilization. This was, of course, far more true in the relatively empty and unsophisticated world of the eighteenth century. Today on oceans teeming with merchant ships and under constant surveillance by satellite and other electronic devices, one was never as isolated as the vulnerable little HMS *Bounty*. Nevertheless, as the morning's events had so dramatically demonstrated a ship at sea was, well, a ship at sea.

'No e-mails; no mobile; not even the most primitive ship's radio,' he said, theatrically. 'Nowadays the Tahitian authorities would have sent a helicopter or a gunboat and the mutineers would have been subdued with stun-guns and taken away to face the international law of the sea. Even in the middle of the Atlantic or Pacific oceans the odds are that there is another vessel within an hour or so even if it's only a Liberian registered container ship or a Taiwanese oil tanker. But back then you were well and truly on your own. And, incidentally, despite everything that has happened in the last century or so this is still a very lonely and vulnerable place to be.'

At this point he always stared around the audience hoping to instil a moment of fear and awe but knowing only too well that the swaying curtain behind him and the memories of a gargantuan alcohol-fuelled lunch behind them and of a similarly proportioned tea in prospect would be enough to lull his listeners into a sense of security however false. Besides, many of them, if not actually asleep, were certainly not paying proper attention.

At home in his lecture room at the University of Wessex on the Casterbridge campus he would have allowed himself the luxury of a snide sarcasm, but here in front of an audience of paying punters he was not as much in charge as he would have wished. He was not exactly a member of the crew but he certainly wasn't a professor addressing a bunch of students. This audience was composed of paying customers and since they paid the piper they called the tune. At home he would have been seriously rude at the expense of a sleeping student; on board ship he was compelled to allow the sleepers to snore on.

After forty minutes or so he stopped and invited questions. This was a risky enterprise. Sometimes the ship's bore moved in and droned on for minutes on end, not asking a question but simply enjoying the sound of his own voice. It was usually *his* but sometimes *hers*. In his experience there was no sexual discrimination when it came to narcolepsy. On marginally less boring occasions an 'expert' of some kind stepped up and contradicted something Tudor had said. Sometimes these people were ignorant cranks with bees in their bonnets; on other sometimes embarrassing occasions they knew more than he did. Best, under those circumstances, to put your hands up and surrender.

This time it was little Umlaut. Tudor hadn't noticed him, sitting there at the back unobtrusively, in the classic position of the man who doesn't want to be recognized, identified, called upon to speak. He was in the aisle seat of the person who wishes to escape without being called upon to do anything. Anonymity seeped from every pore. Yet the diffidence was oddly unnatural. Tudor had seldom met a man who was so obviously confident in himself.

'This morning,' said Umlaut, with assumed diffidence, '*Heute morgen*. Something happened. Very mysterious. Quite alarming. May you please tell us what precisely took place?'

'I'm terribly sorry,' said Tudor, surprised and a little discomfited, 'but I'm really here to talk about the Mutiny on the *Bounty*. I'm afraid today's events just aren't within my remit.'

'Forgive me, but were today's events not a little reminiscent of the events concerning Captain Bligh and Mr Christian?'

He had a funny way of talking, thought Tudor. It was a little like listening to dialogue written by a thriller writer whose first language was not actually English. Tudor had someone in mind but could not for the moment remember who it was. He knew several thriller writers like that.

'I really can't comment,' said Tudor. 'But you seem to know something that the rest of us do not and perhaps you would care to share that information. In what sense were today's events reminiscent of the Mutiny on the *Bounty*, Doctor Umlaut? I think we should be told.'

The little doctor looked shifty and Tudor realized that he hadn't expected his name to be known, much less called out in public.

'Private information,' he said, unconvincingly. 'I have private information that as we are outside national waters and therefore subject to no national jurisdiction but only the law of the sea, you were called in to advise on the legality of a complicated and delicate situation. No?'

'No,' said Tudor, 'or rather no comment. However on the matter of legality and jurisdiction I believe that you're mistaken. When a criminal matter arises in international waters it is treated as if the case had arisen in the country in which the vessel concerned is registered. As you know many ships today are registered, as a matter of convenience, in countries such as Liberia or Panama where justice and the law is administered with, how shall I put it, a somewhat lighter touch than some of us are used to. Luckily, however, the ship on which we have the good fortune to sail is registered in Southampton. Therefore, any misdemeanours that occur on board will be treated as if they had taken place in Great Britain itself. Malefactors will be dealt with according to Her Majesty's law. This applied, of course, to HMS *Bounty* herself. When finally apprehended those mutineers who did not evade the long hand of Brtish justice were brought back to Blighty, tried in properly constituted courts martial and, for the most part, hanged from the yard arms of His Majesty's ships at Spithead. We take a more enlightened view these days, I'm happy to say, but now if you'll excuse me I'm afraid we're completely out of time and in fairness to the macramé class, which is scheduled to begin in only five minutes, I must wind up. Thank you for coming and I look forward to seeing you at my next lecture.

'Sod!' he said to himself, as he acknowledged the slightly half-hearted clapping. 'Try not to sound so pompous.' He knew it was a failing. When rattled, he succumbed to verbal diaorrhea, used long words where short ones would do and generally banged on. He knew instinctively that he should shut up and sit down but something in his nature made him long-winded and patronizing. He did himself no favours.

'Alpha until the questions,' said a voice at his elbow.

It was Elizabeth, grinning with the insubordinate affection he found so beguiling.

'To be honest,' he said, 'I wasn't expecting questions. Brits are usually too embarrassed. It's an American thing, running up to the microphone as soon as the speaker's finished and telling him he knows nothing.'

'Australians do it,' she said. 'We're not shy either. It's a completely British thing that false modesty. I find it rather unattractive. As you know.'

'Yes, I know,' he said, 'but Doctor Umlaut is German.'

The audience had vanished as if by magic and they were alone on stage. The only person in sight but not earshot was the sound technician in his box of tricks at the far end of the auditorium.

'German extraction,' she said. 'He hasn't lived in Germany since he was a child. He's from Leipzig. His family came out soon after the Russians moved in. He owns an island or two, but if he lives anywhere he seems to live on board ship. Useful tax dodge I imagine, and the communications are presumably excellent.'

'What exactly does he do?' Tudor wanted to know. His young protégée seemed to know practically everything there was to know about the German-sounding doctor.

She shrugged. 'Arms, property, drugs, second-hand cars, prostitution.' She sighed. 'That's what I suspect. In other words nothing nice. But it won't show up anywhere. All the paperwork will prove that he is a perfectly above-board banker of some kind. Assets, acquisitions . . . legalized gambling with other people's money. Making squillions out of ordinary people's life savings. Shunting money around so that it breeds. You know my opinion of men like Umlaut.'

'It's called capitalism,' said Tudor, mildly irritated, because once upon a time he too had had scruples and ideals and now he feared they had just become jealousy and suppressed rage. He didn't see why, in a just society, good university lecturers such as himself shouldn't inherit the earth. But somehow they didn't and it was all left to shysters like Umlaut. Never mind, he would never be able to pass through a needle and attain the Kingdom of God.

Elizabeth jabbed him playfully in the ribs.

'You know you don't believe that for a moment. You think it's theft just the same as I do.'

'No matter,' he said. 'It doesn't much matter what we think of him, nor how he makes his money. What was he getting at when he asked those strange questions? Why did he ask them in front of everyone else? Does he know something we don't?'

'You mean, is he in on the plot?'

Tudor thought for a moment. 'I suppose I do,' he said. 'I mean there are two ways of looking at this morning's fiasco. Either it was just a lot of scatterbrained Irish students indulging in an elaborate sort of rag-week stunt, or it was something altogether more significant and sinister which simply mis-fired.'

'We don't know that it's misfired,' said Elizabeth.

'What do you mean by that?'

'The voyage isn't over yet,' she said. 'We have three or four days before we hit New York. We're only halfway through the mystery.'

'But they're locked up,' he protested.

'That's only a key-turn. Just as easy to unlock as to lock.'

'That's silly,' he said.

'I wish I shared your certainty,' she said. 'I think there's more to this than meets the eye. I didn't care for Umlaut's questioning whatever the subtext is. I'm not happy about the captain's laryngitis. I'm deeply suspicious of half the passengers. I think we're all at risk and frankly I'd rather be safe back home in the good old U of W.'

Tudor smiled at her.

'There's absolutely nothing to worry about,' he said, wishing he felt as certain as he sounded. 'As long as I'm here representing law 'n' order and intellectual rigour we have nothing to fear.'

He glanced up at the ceiling and cocked an ear for noises off.

'You know,' he said, 'unless I'm much mistaken the storm has abated and the tempest past. All sounds calm. The worst is behind us. Why don't we go outside and take another turn on deck and see if the waters arc as placid as I sense?'

She stared at him as if he were deranged. Which she sometimes thought he was.

'All right,' she said, at last, 'why not?'

14

The water had become placid as the proverbial mill pond. Extraordinary, mused Tudor, how the sea could move in moments from gurly and growly to butter-wouldn't-melt-in-my-mouth. One moment the depths were all menace, the next they were stroke-your-brow-and-hold-my-hand. The wind had dropped and there were no whitecaps. All was quiet and calm. You could have sculled across this ocean in a skiff.

'Sail ho!' exclaimed a breathy voice just behind them.

Tudor and Elizabeth turned abruptly and saw Mandy Goldslinger in a Florida female approximation of a sailor suit. She wore white trousers and a white jacket, with much gold braid, buttons, epaulettes and a blue belt tightly buckled. She looked like the runner up in the best first mate competition, senior section. She smelt vaguely as if she had been drinking margaritas, swayed slightly despite the new calm but was tipsy rather than drunk.

'Sail ho!' she repeated loudly and liltingly in what she must have thought was a good imitation of a cry from the crow's nest. As she called out she gesticulated in the direction of a distant horizon and when Tudor and Elizabeth followed her outstretched hand with their eyes they were surprised to see a shape. It was not merely a ship shape but also, as the cruise director suggested, a ship under sail. A lot of it. Billowing in the prescribed manner.

'A ship,' said Cornwall fatuously.

'Not any old ship, darling,' said Mandy, 'a barquentine no less. Four masts, the tallest little short of two hundred and thirty feet; the most forward square-rigged and the three behind rigged fore and aft. I'd judge that she carries the best part of, oh I'd say around thirty-six thousand square feet of sail, and she's something over two thousand tons and about three hundred and sixty feet long. Modern, very. Judging from the way she sails I'd say she was built in Belgium possibly in the Langerbrugge Yard in Ghent. But I'd say she was registered in Luxembourg, though Swedish owned. Can't be much more than ten years old. Ask me another.'

She smiled in triumph.

'You're making it up,' said Elizabeth, visibly impressed.

'*Au contraire*,' said Mandy. 'But I'll admit we've had the bins on her from the bridge.

And that wondrous display of sail doesn't entirely account for the speed she's making. That's from her twelve cylinder diesel engine which generates thirteen hundred and fifty horsepower with seven to one reduction gear operating a four-blade variable-pitch aluminium/ bronze propeller that gives a speed of twelve knots — '

'Stop, stop!' said Tudor. 'My ears are bleeding.'

Ms Goldslinger laughed, a husky tinkling sound much practised and rehearsed.

'You didn't know my alter ego was Jane of *Jane's Ships*, did you? Don't worry. She's an old friend; *Star Clipper*. Klaus or Jurgen is at the wheel. They're twins so can't tell them apart. And my friend Jeffrey Rayner's on board. He says they have a surprise for us and when Jeffrey says 'surprise' he means *surprise*.'

'Like what?' Tudor wanted to know.

'He wouldn't say. Surprisingly shtumm. I thought we'd pay a visit in one of the Zodiacs. Want to come?'

Tudor glanced at the girl with a raised interrogative eyebrow and she nodded back.

'We'll give you life jackets, but I'd wear something waterproof. Warm too. It may look calm and not very far but mid-Atlantic in an open boat gets kinda choppy and chilly.'

Mandy smiled a wintry smile at Elizabeth. If looks could kill this wouldn't quite have done the job but it would certainly have maimed. Or frozen. It was the coolness rather than the ferocity that was marked. Elizabeth smiled back but her eyes were almost as glacial as the cruise director's.

Five minutes later the two guests were back in yellow woolly hats decorated, slightly improbably, with the logo of the University of Wessex. They also wore anoraks. Mandy Goldslinger in a figure-hugging *Duchess* weatherproof catsuit looked superior and ushered them slinkily to a rope ladder suspended from a door several decks down. At the bottom a black inflatable bobbed dangerously alongside with three crew members lounging nonchalantly in charge. Just as they were about to set off they were joined by two thirty-something men in black wet suits. Neither Tudor nor Elizabeth recognized them. They nodded curtly. Presumably, thought Tudor, they were security officers of some sort or another. He wondered who exactly was in charge. He vaguely assumed it was Mandy Goldslinger though he wasn't entirely sure.

It was a bumpy ride. The boat's rubber bottom slapped the water as the skipper revved the show-off outboards in a display of nautical muscle-flexing. From high up on the *Duchess* the ocean looked oily and placid; down here it felt rough as stubble. As the *Duchess* receded so she began to look more and more like a stylized child's toy safely at anchor in a bath tub. Conversely, as the four-masted barquentine got closer and closer she looked more and more like the real thing. She gleamed like a well-trained thoroughbred in the paddock and if you hadn't known that she was a creature of the twentieth century with the gear to match you would have suspected her of being a close blood relation of the *Cutty Sark* bringing home tea from China at a rate of wind-blown knots.

A flight of wooden steps had been lowered over the side of the ship and two blond able-bodied seamen were standing at the bottom ready to assist the passengers' landing. Mandy Goldslinger and Elizabeth went first, armed expertly from taut rubber to polished teak and followed closely by Tudor and the two wet-suits. At the head of this collapsible staircase stood an epauletted, white-haired skipper in tropical drill and a dapper figure in white canvas trousers, espadrilles and a striped Breton jerkin whom Tudor supposed to be Mandy's friend Jeffrey Rayner. As she kissed him full on the lips Tudor felt his suspicions confirmed.

As he stepped gingerly on to the wooden deck Mandy introduced him to Rayner and the Captain who apparently had a German name that Tudor did not quite catch.

'Jeffrey and the captain have one of our boats,' said Mandy.

'I didn't know that one of our boats was missing,' said Tudor.

The wet-suits had vanished.

'No reason why you should,' said Mandy. 'Boat overboard!' She honked a brassy laugh and stopped abruptly when no one else joined in. 'Well,' she said, 'that's not a usual cry on board ship. On the other hand, our boat must have gone overboard and you'd think someone would have seen it and raised an alarm.'

There was a longish silence.

'Seems to me,' said Elizabeth, 'that almost anything could disappear overboard on a big ship like ours without anyone noticing.'

Mandy Goldslinger went quickly into PR mode, assisted by the obvious fact that she disliked Elizabeth Burney very much, 'The crew on the *Duchess* is highly trained to detect and report the slightest irregularity at all times and in all places,' she said.

'Oh come on, Mandy,' said Tudor, 'you know that isn't true. It can't be. It's half a mile at least just to walk round the

Promenade Deck. And at night when it's dark and there are virtually no outside lights, you simply couldn't see an object go over the side. And in anything more than a slight breeze you wouldn't hear it either.'

'Just a little plop as it hit the surface,' said Elizabeth. 'Plop. Then vanish never to be seen again. Easy peasy.'

'Yes,' said Mandy, 'well.' And she took out a cigarette and lit it. The captain asked her to put it out. She did, but looked furious.

'So what exactly happened?' asked Tudor. 'I mean you were just sailing along and suddenly you saw one of our lifeboats in the middle of the Atlantic.'

'Well no.' Rayner looked bothered. He and the captain had decided it was unwise to say too much on open insecure lines but now they were all together in, as it were, private, they felt secure enough to reveal that there was another ship involved. The barquentine had spotted this before they were aware of the *Duchess* lifeboat. Indeed had it not been for the presence of the larger vessel they might not have seen the lifeboat at all. She was an elderly rust-bucket of the sort that seemed to sink periodically and usually east of Suez and, thought Tudor, nearly always full of pilgrims *en route* to the Haj. But hush, that was prejudice. Rayner and the captain reckoned

148

she was a retired cross-channel steamer of some description. She was flying an Irish flag and bore the name *Michael Collins* on her bows and stern as well as the unlikely claim to be registered in the landlocked African republic of Chad.

All attempts to establish contact with the ship failed totally. The *Michael Collins* did not respond to shouts on the loudhailer, flags sending semaphore signals, an Aldis lamp flickering Morse Code and, least of all, to anything to do with electronics. Jeffrey Rayner had tapped her name into Google on one of the barquentine's computers and had discovered that she was some sort of floating university campus.

'Based in Limerick,' said the Captain.

'Some sort of self-proclaimed Institution for the Study of — '

'World Republicanism,' chipped in Tudor and Elizabeth, speaking in unison.

Mandy Goldslinger looked long-suffering but unsurprised. The captain and Jeffrey Rayner exchanged glances. They had never previously heard of such a thing and it obviously sounded as bogus to them as it had previously done to Tudor and Elizabeth.

'Ashley Carpenter strikes again,' said Tudor. 'Originally I assumed this was cock-up, but I'm beginning to wonder if it might not be conspiracy after all. Mind if I have a look at the boat?'

No one objected. The lifeboat had been taken on board and was sitting on the after-deck alongside the swimming-pool and looking like some sort of beached fish. It was out of its element and far from home.

Tudor clambered in. There was a brownish stain on the port side just where there was a hole in the side presumably for a rowlock, though the lifeboat had a moderately powerful inboard engine. The *Duchess* lifeboats were carefully maintained so there should have been no need to row.

'Blood?' asked Tudor, staring hard at the stain.

'We assumed so,' said the captain.

'What exactly happened?' asked Tudor, frowning knowledgeably at the supposed bloodstain.

It wasn't entirely clear what 'exactly' happened because the whole incident was so murky. *Star Clipper* had been bowling along, minding her own business and doing her inimitable greyhound-of-the-sea act when they had stumbled, as it were, on the SS *Michael Collins*, doing something furtive with the *Duchess*'s lifeboat which appeared to be tied up alongside. As soon as the *Michael Collins* realized that the sailing ship was keen to establish what was going on, the old Afro-Irish ship turned tail and scuttled off.

Tudor listened attentively to what the two men had to say and, at the same time, paced up and down the wooden lifeboat not entirely sure what he was looking for, not at all sure what exactly was going on, but uneasily aware that he himself was a part of what was happening.

The boat was essentially open and undecked, designed to take between thirty and forty survivors who would have been packed tightly on the plank-like seats. She may have been a seaworthy craft but she was primitive. There were two lockers in the bows, one on which side, secured only by doors with only rudimentary latches such as you might find in any old country cottage. Without knowing quite why he was doing so Tudor opened one of these doors and felt inside. His hand encountered something squared off and brick-like. He grasped it and lifted it out. It was cold and metallic and, as he stared at it thoughtfully, he heard Elizabeth cry out, 'That's gold. You've struck gold!'

And after he had handed it to her and knelt down to look inside the locker he realized that he had indeed struck gold, for there, packed neatly in the compartment where he had expected to find life-jackets or torches or iron rations, were a great many ingots, stacked neatly as logs in a fire-basket.

'Finders keepers,' he said, softly and facetiously.

It was a veritable treasure trove.

On inspecting a sample ingot Tudor was pleased to find that, as he suspected, the letters GR were stamped on the base. To the uninitiated this might have suggested 'George Rex' and indicated an English king called George. Tudor knew, however, that it merely indicated that the gold had been supplied by his old sparring partner Guy Roberts, now knighted and therefore 'Sir' Guy but better known as 'Golden Balls', 'Mr Goldbar', 'Goldilocks' or any one of a number of similar sobriquets involving the precious metal.

Guy was an Eton and Oxford-educated smoothie who had unexpectedly gone into the world of gold-trading which was traditionally dominated by Essex-boy traders in leather jackets. Guy had taken this world by storm to such an extent that within a decade he was the world's leading expert on the subject.

One of his stocks-in-trade was supplying gold bars to the mega-rich as an insurance against fluctuations in markets of all kinds. He gave billionaires the chance of the plutocratic equivalent of hiding used fivers under the mattress or the stair carpet. His clients were men such as Umlaut or Prince Abdullah and he offered them a rainy-day safety net. The Umlauts and Abdullahs of this world avoided tax by having their offices and headquarters in a floating tax haven. The naïve pirates from the Emerald Isle had come up with the luck of the Irish. Stumbling on this sort of treasure trove was a brilliant fluke. But being flukey didn't make it less brilliant.

15

The lifeboat and the gold ingots returned to the *Duchess* whence, presumably, they had come. No one aboard the *Star Clipper* seemed distressed by their departure; indeed they seemed relieved to be rid of them.

'So what do you make of that?' asked Elizabeth, as they clambered back on board the cruise ship. Turning back on the promenade deck they leaned against the rail and watched the barquentine let out sails and gather speed on her passage towards the Mediterranean. Music of some kind came wafting across the waves. It could have been Van Gelis or something more classical. Distance lent the melody charm and ambiguity.

There was no one else in earshot.

'I've heard of returning to the gold standard,' said Tudor, 'but I never thought I'd see it in practice. How much do you imagine that gold's worth?'

'Ask me another,' said Elizabeth. 'Stocks and shares may break my bones but gold . . .' She shrugged. 'I simply don't know. But that's a lot of gold. A hundred ingots, do you think? And whatever else gold keeps its price. Safer than houses. Maybe not as spectacular as a shrewd property investment or Princess Margaret's jewellery but as safe as, well, houses.'

'Safer than bricks and mortar, wouldn't you say?'

Tudor frowned into the gathering gloom.

'I'd say they were kilo bars. And if you're talking about two hundred pounds an ounce, which I guess you are, then each bar is worth about seven grand, I would have thought we were looking at at least five hundred bars which would add up to around three and a half million quid. Not a lot these days but a useful stand-by for moments of need. Better than a piggy bank.' This was unexpected.

'You what?' He was taken by surprise. One minute she professed complete ignorance and the next she came up with some arcane remark which indicated exactly the reverse. Maddening woman.

'I'd say that the gold bars in that lifeboat add up to about three and a half million quid.'

The information hung in the salty air like a corpse waiting for dissection. A skilful forensic wielding of the scalpel should carve out some missing secrets. In clumsy hands, however, the knife might reveal nothing at all.

'So,' said Tudor thoughtfully, 'you're telling me that one of the *Duchess*'s lifeboats went AWOL in the middle of the night with three and a half million pounds of gold ingots on board. It fetches up against an unlikely floating college of an equally improbable Irish university which is surprised by our elegant flying greyhound of the sea. The Irish rustbucket does a bunk and the boat fetches up with Jeffrey and his pals with the loot intact but no human occupant and a sinister-looking bloodstain on board.'

'*Presumed* bloodstain,' said Elizabeth sharply. 'We don't know it was blood and we've no way of proving it one way or the other. Not until we reach New York.'

'I don't want to wait till New York; I want to solve this at sea. As you say — one way or another. I don't trust any police force to get this one right. Least of all the Americans.'

Like many Englishmen he was sceptical about American expertise while actually having very little real first-hand experience of it. He was prejudiced and convinced of his own skills. Sometimes this self-confidence was justified and sometimes not. On this occasion he did not have to compete with any form of official police force but on the other hand he had some experienced opposition from among his fellow passengers. He was almost forgetting Sir Goronwy Watkyn and the former CID inspector, Freddie Grim. No doubt also senior members of the *Duchess*'s crew would also want their penny-worth. He would have to move fast for all sorts of reasons. In a sense, too, he already had an excess of evidence and a surfeit of information: idiotic Irish terrorists in the brig, gold ingots in an abandoned lifeboat, a mysterious bloodstain and a missing captain. It was almost too much.

He was less and less inclined to believe the story of laryngitis explaining the captain's disappearance. A throat infection was too much to swallow in more ways than one. As far as he was concerned the captain was missing. It was not just his voice that was lost.

'You could just wash your hands of the whole thing. Leave it till we dock in New York and let the professionals handle it.'

'I *am* the professional,' he said coldly. 'As you perfectly well know I have a professional reputation to maintain. If we reach the United States with these mysteries unsolved the name of the University of Wessex will be mud.'

Elizabeth did not say what she was thinking which was that sometimes her boss could seem a little absurd. She admired him much of the time and there was no doubting his knowledge and abilities. Sometimes, however, he over-reached himself and she was beginning to wonder whether this might not be one of those occasions.

'Penny for them,' she said, wrinkling her nose and looking quizzical, 'What are your thoughts, oh Mighty One?'

She had the rare knack of being able to send him up without his being irritated. Or, she sometimes thought, even noticing.

'There are only two people on board ship who strike me as being rich enough to have that sort of loot on board. Likewise the same two people are just the sort of oddball, fly-by-night characters who might want to have ready cash in a reliable but disposable form. Your average Goldman Sachs wunderkind wouldn't be on the Gold Standard.'

'But Umlaut or Prince Abdullah might be?'

'What made you think of those two?' Tudor asked, irritably.

'I'm not stupid,' she said. 'Or hadn't you noticed?'

He smiled.

'So whoever was in the lifeboat nicked Umlaut or the Prince's pocket money and was about to transfer it to the Irish university rustbucket when they were surprised by the *Flying Dutchman*.'

'So the thief,' she said, pursing her lips in

thought, 'went aboard the floating Irish ivory tower but left the gold on the lifeboat because he was a guilty thing surprised.'

'Something like that,' agreed Tudor.

'He couldn't have boarded the sailing ship. Jeffrey would have told us. I've known Jeffrey for years. He wouldn't connive in a crime like that. Not any sort of crime actually. Straight as a die, Jeffrey.'

'And there's a connection between the abortive hijacking and the theft of the gold bars and the disappearance of the captain,' said Tudor. 'Besides which our mutual friend Ashley Carpenter is involved.'

'So it seems,' she agreed.

'Don't you think we should talk to Umlaut and Abdullah and find out which of them owns the gold?'

This obvious next move was deferred by the sudden arrival of Sir Goronwy Watkyn looking majestic but bothered in a sort of Celtic Merlin mode. His mane of white hair was awry and a black cape fastened with a brass chain at the neck flapped theatrically in the breeze.

'Crime at sea, I understand,' said the old knight. 'Never fear there is no such thing as a perfect crime, especially when Sir Goronwy Watkyn is at hand. Do we have a body?'

'Everything is under control,' said Tudor.

'Not what I hear, dear boy,' said Sir Goronwy patting Tudor's shoulder in a gesture that managed to be both avuncular and threatening, 'Never fear though. Uncle Goronwy will sort everything out.'

'Thank you,' said Tudor, 'but everything is under control and there's no need for anyone else to be bothered.'

'No bother. No bother at all.' The old Celt tossed his head and gazed out at the horizon. 'It's a rare privilege to be able to do in practice what I have spent a lifetime perfecting in theory.'

'It's all right,' said Tudor. 'I've been in communication with all concerned and, as I say, it's under control. There's no need for you to be involved in any way. Just act normally and carry on with the lecturing.'

'What I say now.' The old man lowered his voice so that his listeners had to strain to catch what he was saying over the sibilant sighing of the sea, 'What I always say is *Cherchez le pied.*' He beamed with self-satisfaction.

'You sure you don't mean *cherchez la femme,*' said Elizabeth, a little obviously.

'Certainly not!' he said with asperity, '*Cherchez* chiropody, if one is being alliterative. The answer lies in the feet. People tell palms or look for character in a person's face but I tell you now that the solutions to practically everything may be found below the ankle. Just mark my words. I concede that this is a discovery I have made late in life but it is none the less valid for being belated.'

He inclined his head in an old-fashioned thespian manner and seemed on the verge of clicking his heels and kissing Elizabeth's hand. At the last moment however he seemed to think better of it and simply turned and disappeared indoors.

'Silly old phoney!' said Tudor.

'I suppose so,' said Elizabeth. She frowned. 'And talking of feet I'm afraid PC Plod is heading our way.'

It was indeed Grim, the unlikely lay-reader, formerly of the Metropolitan Police who was heading their way. His appearance lived up to his surname. He looked serious and forbidding in a curmudgeonly disobliging sort of way. Not at all the expression you'd expect to find on the face of a lay preacher on a Sunday after matins.

'I've had words with the First Officer, Cornwall,' said Freddie, 'And I take an exceedingly dim view. It seems to my good self that you have abrogated an entirely inappropriate level of responsibility in the matter of what appears to be prima facie an act of piracy on the High Seas. What have you got to say for yourself?'

'I have nothing to say for myself,' said Tudor, 'I simply don't know what you're talking about. And when you say 'First Officer' to whom are you referring?'

'Angus Donaldson, of course. As well you know.'

'Forgive me, Freddie,' said Tudor in a friendly familiar fashion which was calculated to infuriate, 'but Donaldson's actual title is Staff Captain and he's not in charge. The boss is Captain Hardy, the Master.'

'The Master is, as you well know, indisposed. Not even I have been able to make contact with him. In view of this, er, indisposition Angus Donaldson is in charge whether he is First Officer or Staff Captain. Captain Donaldson has told me something of what appears to have taken place and was much relieved when I explained details of my former life and qualifications. From now on I am in charge and you can cease whatever activities you have been indulging in. From what I am able to glean from Captain Donaldson this is a case for the professionals.'

'I'm not actually entirely certain about that,' said Tudor. 'With the greatest possible respect to your former life and all that I rather had the impression that you had retired and moved on to what might aptly described as higher things.'

'This is no time for facetiousness,' said Grim, who never had time for facetiousness of any kind. 'An attempt has been made to hijack this ship in the middle of the ocean and I understand there has also been an attempt at theft or robbery involving a stolen lifeboat and a mysterious vessel now vanished.'

'The lifeboat I can assure you is safely recovered and back on board together with its cargo or whatever it was.'

'Whatever it was indeed,' said the former inspector, pouncing on the phrase as if it was a fugitive from justice that he was about to apprehend with a snap of his official handcuffs. 'Whatever was it?'

'I would have thought Captain Donaldson would have told you whatever it was if he had indeed entrusted the enquiry to you. I mean, I hate to pull rank and all that, but (a) the Captain who, as we all know is Sam Hardy, Master of the *Duchess* is in charge, and (b) I am already involved in this affair *faute de mieux*.'

'Don't try and bamboozle me with fancy frog phrases,' said Grim. 'I may not be a professor but that doesn't make me stupid.'

But before this conversation could degenerate further they were interrupted. It was

Mandy Goldslinger looking alarmed and dishevelled.

'Gentlemen, gentlemen,' she said breathlessly, 'I need your help. Something's happened.'

16

'What do you mean 'something's happened'?'

Tudor took Mandy Goldslinger by the elbow and pulled her out of earshot. He did not want Grim to overhear. Elizabeth was doing a good job of blocking the former policeman while attempting merely to seem flirty and ingratiating.

'It's your ring-leaderene,' shouted Mandy, in a stage-shriek designed to rise above the wail of the waves and the sigh of the sea. 'She's escaped. Vanished. Done a bunk. She's at large. Somewhere on board ship. Dangerous. Maybe armed.'

'What?' asked Tudor semi-rhetorically. '*Tipperary Tatler*? How so? Who let her out?'

La Goldslinger sighed. 'Classic cock-up,' she said. 'Your Irish captives asked for refreshment. The infinitely civilised British acquiesced. Jeez, you Brits. Cup of tea, Mr Bin Laden? Absolutely. Earl Grey or Lapsang Souchong? No problem. Milk? Sugar? So that's what happened. Little stewardess is sent in to the prisoners with a tray of tea and cucumber sandwiches. I speak metaphorically but only just. She is hit on head. Again, I speak metaphorically. Your friend the flame-haired temptress from Tipperary takes her outfit and exits left with a load of empties. Hey fucking presto she's part of the crew. Every girl who carries a tray on board this ship is bog-Irish or fake Filipino. No one knows who they are. Your girl is just part of the herd.'

'You're telling me that the leader of a gang of international pirates has been captured and locked up only to be allowed to walk free without any let or hindrance?'

'Seems about the size of it,' said Mandy.

'You mentioned tea,' said Tudor glancing at his watch. 'I could do with a cup. Maybe a cucumber sandwich.' He glanced back at Grim. 'In private.'

'OK,' she said. 'Butler's Pantry in ten minutes. I'll make sure we have a quiet table to ourselves.'

She left, presumably to arrange tea and Tudor returned to his long-suffering sidekick and the aggrieved Grim.

'Look, Freddie,' he said, laying an ingratiating hand on the ex-copper's shoulder, 'There really isn't any need for you to be involved, not least because there's nothing to be involved, as it were *in*.' He laughed, aware that he was sounding donnish. 'Naturally if there *is* anything to be involved in you'll be the first person to be, well, involved. But right now there's nothing whatever to worry about. I've been thinking about your sermon too. Very thought provoking if I may say so.'

'The Lord moves in mysterious ways,' said Grim. 'Me, too. You'll never know where I'll turn up next or in what guise. Just like our Lord. He is everywhere and nowhere. Now you see Him; now you don't. You would be well advised not to sup with the Devil even using a long spoon. Best, by far, to stay alongside your old pal Freddie.'

Tudor had never noticed quite how yellow Freddie's teeth were when he smiled. Nor how bad his breath. Perhaps the mouth had deteriorated since leaving the force.

'I'll think about it Freddie,' he said, 'but really, there's no need for concern. Sam Hardy runs a tight ship. None of us will come to any harm while he's in charge.'

'Tight,' said Freddie, 'is the operative word. Sam Hardy is a drunk, as well you know. Ho, ho and a bottle of rum is not just a figure of speech in his case. Speaking as one who hasn't touched a drop of the hard stuff since I went on the wagon many years ago I know of what I speak.'

'Well . . . ' began Tudor, but Grim silenced him with a finger to his mouth. 'Say no more,' he said. 'You know where to find me if you need professional help.'

It was on the tip of Tudor's tongue to say something clever and superior but he thought better of it and said nothing, simply stared out to sea for a moment, then said to the precocious Elizabeth, 'Why don't you ferret around while I have a cucumber sandwich and a cup of Earl Grey with la Goldslinger? I'll see you in a cabin later.'

'OK,' she said, grinning. 'We don't have ferrets in Tasmania but I think I know what you're saying. I'll sniff around.'

'Unobtrusively,' he said.

She smirked back at him. 'Obtrusive? *Moi*? I'll be discreet as the day is long. I'll be virtually invisible. No one will have the first idea of what I'm doing.'

'Not just a pretty face, are you?'

'On the contrary,' She was still smirking. 'That's exactly what I'll be. Just a pretty face. Plus pert breasts, fine cheekbones, a neat bum, long legs and an almost tiny waist. Combine all those and everyone will think I'm here for ornament only. That's the way of the world. I shall pass without notice.'

'That'll be the day,' Tudor spoke with feeling.

They both went indoors, she, on a predatory prowl; he for a cuppa in the Butler's Pantry.

When he arrived he wondered, not for the first time, who was fooling who and why. What was the thinking behind a scene like this? Who had originally thought of the idea of taking the Ritz to sea? Whose bright idea was it to recreate the Palm Court complete with tinkling tea-cups and crustless egg sandwiches and crustless cucumber sandwiches and crustless smoked salmon sandwiches, scones and strawberry jam and cream, miniature swiss rolls and miniature sausage rolls and miniature jam tarts and Dundee Cake. 'Dundee Cake.' He seemed to remember Cary Grant rolling the words off his tongue in some old Hitchcock movie just before biting into a slice of said cake and rolling that round his tongue instead of words. Come to that why wasn't Cary Grant sitting at a table being charming to some old duck who was spending her late husband's legacy? Or more likely yet, why wasn't Cary Grant out on the dance floor schmoozing round with another elderly widow with money to spend on afternoon tea in the Butler's Pantry? What was that story about Cary Grant? The one about the newspaper reporter who cabled the film star in connection with a feature he was writing and simply sent a message saying 'How old Cary Grant?' to which Grant replied, quick as a flash, 'Old Cary Grant fine. How you?' Palms. They even had palm trees weaving gently in the wind to the sounds of Strauss, or was it Offenbach being scratched out by the trio of young Latvians or Lithuanians from the conservatoire on some Baltic beach. And talking of Cary Grant, he recognized the fellow in the off-white linen suit shuffling round the dance floor and shouting into the hearing-aid of his blue-rinsed partner as he executed a nimble 'one-two-three, one-two-three, one-two-three' which would have more than passed muster at any *thé dansant* in any palais from Shanghai to Shoreham. It was Ambrose Perry, the gentleman host. There should have been 'Let them eat cake,' he muttered to himself: Battenburg, Pontefract, simnel, Victoria sponge, Dundee dammit. He could murder an eclair or what they used to call soap cakes at school in cricket matches when the headmaster's wife did the honours with the huge chipped urn and the huge chipped tea-pots and . . .

'Are you all right, sir? May I be of any assistance?' It was a waiter in striped trousers and black jacket doing a passable imitation of a landlubber maitre d' at the Ritz.

'All right?' said Tudor, aware that Mandy Goldslinger was waving at him from a far corner of the pantry where she had secured an isolated table for two in a secluded corner. It wasn't quite screened off, but Ms

Goldslinger's haughty demeanour and icy stare was more than enough to repel boarders.

'You looked, if I may say so, sir,' said the waiter doing a plausible Jeeves imitation, 'a little under the weather.'

It was increasingly rare to find a genuine waiter on a cruise ship these days. Even the gentlemen hosts were more host-like than gentlemanly. Only the officer class were British. The other ranks were mostly all foreign. Tudor heard his inner voice saying these things and was horrified. He sounded like his father.

'No, I'm fine, thank you,' said Tudor.

'You still look a little green,' said the waiter, 'and feverish. I think you may be running a temperature. Perspiration on the brow. I hope we're not about to be struck by one of those bugs. The *Duchess* has been bug-free for as long as I've been on board but, as you say, there's always a first time.'

'Thank you. Thank you,' said Tudor. 'Not to worry. Really.'

'You kept repeating something about Dundee cake,' said the waiter. 'It's not a standard item, but as you're with Miss Goldslinger I'm sure some can be arranged. May I fetch you Dundee cake?'

'Thank you, no,' said Tudor. 'But water

171

would be good. A glass of water.'

'Certainly, sir. Sparkling or still? Ice? Lemon or lime?'

'Just water, thanks. And, er . . . thanks.'

He looked at the man suspiciously. He was too good to be true.

'You all right?' Mandy Goldslinger had changed into a curious tea-drinking outfit — a sort of black lamé cat-suit with a high collar. More Vegas than vicarage.

'I'm fine. I wish people would stop suggesting otherwise.'

'You don't look fine. You look ill. Would you like brandy?'

'The man's bringing me water.'

'The man's Shane. Been with the ship for years. Queen of the Butler's Pantry. He's from Toowoomba in Queensland. Cute,eh? Surprised you hadn't noticed him already.'

'Must have been on shore leave whenever I've been on before,' said Tudor.

She poured Earl Grey from a silvery teapot.

'This'll put the hair back on your chest,' she said. 'Twining's best. We had Sam Twining himself on board once, showing us how to do a proper brew. A lot depends on the water. We have special tea water just for the Pantry. Malvern I believe. Just like Her Majesty. Did you know that your Queen

Elizabeth takes bottles of Malvern Water wherever she goes? Especially for brewing afternoon tea. We have royal authors on board regularly. That's one thing they all agree on.'

Tudor felt very tired. He put a hand to his head.

'You don't have to do a sales pitch for me, Mandy,' he said, 'I've read the brochure. I've heard Sam Hardy doing his spiel.'

Her mood changed.

'I need to talk to you about Sam,' she said, sounding serious and almost human.

'Yes,' he said.

Shane of Toowoomba shimmered over with the glass of water which he deposited deftly on the table in text-book manner with the non-carrying hand crooked behind his back. He smiled synthetically. All very Butler's Pantry, thought Tudor, still wondering at the incongruity of it all. The ship bumped, reminding him that they were still at sea.

'I'm worried about Sam.'

'Yes,' said Tudor. He was not in the mood to be helpful.

'You see,' she said, 'Sam and me.' She now sounded coy, almost girlish. Tudor wondered if this was an act like everything else about her.

'The truth is,' she continued, 'that Sam and me — Sam and I that is — we, the two of us, are an item. We're an item. That is we, if you see what I mean. Sam and I are, like, together. We're an item. Except that the company has a rule about members of crew you know, well, we have to pretend. When we're on board together. Everyone's been, well, you know, very British about us, but if the company found out one of us would have to go.'

'I see,' said Tudor, not really seeing. He would have been surprised by this revelation if he had been particularly interested but he wasn't. He didn't care about Mandy's private life. Nor the Captain's. He wasn't really into private lives, he thought ruefully. Perhaps that was his problem.

'So why are you worried?' he asked, sipping his water.

'Because I can't find him. And I can't get into his cabin. The lock's been changed so my key doesn't work.'

17

The Baltic strings were playing a polka. Tudor
could imagine lads and lasses in some
northern Tivoli strutting their stuff under the
larches in summer dusk while an orchestra on
a wooden nineteenth century bandstand
oompahed out a number such as this.
Ambrose Perry and his colleagues and
partners did not, however, strut or trip the
light fantastic. Instead they swayed gently and
shuffled around the floor making sure their
lady-passengers remained upright and followed them more or less in time to the music.
It was, in its way, an impressive performance.
Tudor thought of flying buttresses holding up
an ancient abbey and was impressed enough
by the metaphor to make a mental note to
use it in a paper for a learned journal at some
future date.

'An item,' he said. 'You and Sam Hardy.
The two of you.'

Like royalty, he often, when nonplussed,
repeated the remark just vouchsafed, if
necessary more than once. It gave him
valuable thinking time.

'Yes,' said Ms Goldslinger, dabbing at her

mascara with a frilly handkerchief. 'Sam and me. The two of us. An item.'

Royal-speak was catching.

On the far side of the dance floor Tudor could see Prince Abdullah and his harem. The Prince was not smoking as the Butler's Pantry was a smoke-free zone. Instead he was glowering around a cucumber sandwich. The wives poured him tea, fed him food and generally fawned. Tudor wondered idly how many there were and whether they had particular duties or rosters — toenail cutting wife, a nostril hair-removing wife, a Scotch-pouring wife. Their eyes sparkled from their almost-all concealing Muslim headdresses and their bodies shimmered seductively under their supposedly chaste robes. He'd be prepared to bet they owed more to Dior or St Laurent than a cut-price couturier in the soukh back home.

'So you've been having it off with the captain.'

Tudor was aware he sounded indelicate.

Mandy Goldslinger blushed to the roots of her hair — which did not exactly match the unsplit ends. Time for a visit to the ship's coiffeuse he thought to himself.

'The physical side of things between Sam and myself is only part of the chemistry between us. We think of ourselves as human beings not like, you know, 'sex toys'.'

'I'm sorry,' he said, 'I didn't mean to imply anything else. But let's, as you say, cut to the chase. You haven't seen Sam Hardy for a while and you can't get into his cabin because it's locked and the locks have been changed.'

'Yup,' she said.

'So who's in charge?' he asked her, expecting her to answer 'Angus Donaldson' which, gratifyingly, she did.

'So did he change the locks?'

'Not personally, no. Angus isn't a DIY person.'

'That's not what I meant. Did he order the locks changed? Is he responsible for Sam's disappearance?'

'I honestly don't know,' she said, looking disturbingly weepy. 'In Sam's absence Angus is the boss.'

'Some people say that Angus is the boss whether Sam is around or not.' Tudor tried not to sound uncharitable. 'Sam is brilliant PR; great Captain Birds Eye. Passengers adore him. He could read tide tables or Lloyd's Log and they'd hang on his every word, but when it comes to actually sailing the ship one isn't quite so sure. In a seafaring sense there are those who think old Sam is past his sell-by date.'

'That's not fair,' said Mandy indignantly.

'He's one of the great sailors as you know perfectly well. He still keeps a Troy on the Fowey River and he sails it himself whenever he can get down to Cornwall.'

'Which isn't often.'

'He's kept very busy. The *Duchess* isn't the *Duchess* without him.'

'Which is now.'

'I don't know,' she said, 'I simply don't know.' She took a mouthful of thin China tea. 'This isn't like him. He's never gone AWOL on a voyage before. Never in all the years I've known him.'

Tudor looked out across the Butler's Pantry like an ancient mariner on the qui-vive for icebergs or albatrosses. Prince Abdullah was still glowering and when Tudor followed his gaze he saw that he was glowering at his arch-enemy Doctor Umlaut who was sitting with his wife at a corner table which had Umlaut all over it. You sensed that this was table Umlauts-for-the-use-of-only and that should any common or garden ordinary passenger try to usurp it they would get short shrift from Shane the maitre d' from Toowoomba. What made Tudor frown almost as menacingly as Prince Abdullah was that there were three at the Umlaut table and the third party was none other than his precocious side-kick and Ph.D. student,

Elizabeth Burney. She seemed relaxed, at ease — as indeed did the Umlauts. It was if they had known each other for years. Tudor was no lip-reader, but from the shapes their mouths were making he would have said they were not speaking English.

Mandy was talking. Tudor wrenched his gaze away from the tableau before him and paid attention to her. She was agitated.

'I've been on the *Duchess* for longer than I care to remember,' she said, 'and every other voyage I've been on has been almost totally without incident. Ocean flat as duckpond; passengers friendly and appreciative; crew efficient and courteous; no serious illness; no more than occasional fatalities and then always from natural causes on account of advanced years and chronic long term illness. The *Duchess* has never had what other ships had: no mystery bugs; no sewage in the staterooms; no bloody pirates. Just cruisy-cruisy. All quiet on the Western Approaches. No man, woman or child overboard. Just what the doctor ordered. Everything always passed off without incident. But this voyage is just one long incident after another. I think there's a Jonah on board.' She narrowed her eyes. 'You're not a Jonah, are you?'

The three girls were now playing the Radetsky March which presumably called for a military two-step. Ambrose Perry and his colleagues and their charges went on shuffling gently just the same. It would take more than a change of tempo from the orchestra to make them break sweat. Besides, if they did there would have been fatalities among the old ladies. Not that there was any sign of stumbling among the dancers. The swell of the ocean beneath was insufficient to cause more than the occasional gentle shift of the goalposts and their pace was so stately that there was no danger of falling.

'I'm a guest speaker in good standing, as well you know,' said Tudor, 'and for all his faults the same is true of Sir Goronwy. I don't think you can be a regular cruiser and Jonah too. So that rules out Prince Abdullah and Doctor Umlaut as well. They're recidivists.'

'I'm not superstitious,' said Mandy, 'but I *am* bothered. This voyage is becoming a nightmare. First we have that mad Irish hijack which is nipped in the bud, but then the ring leader gets sprung. Meanwhile a mysterious Flying Irishman turns up and does a bunk, but not before one of our lifeboats comes alongside her with a cargo of gold bars. And then they're surprised in mid ocean by this bloody great sailing ship. So we get the lifeboat and the gold back but the captain is missing. Or seems to be. Or might be or might not. And whoever was in charge of the lifeboat has vanished. Along with the captain.'

'Unless the person who was in charge of the lifeboat was the captain himself.'

'But why in God's name would Sam make off in a lifeboat with several millions worth of gold bars and then vanish, presumably either overboard or into the bowels of the mad Irish university ship? Which may or may not have your would-be obituarist Professor Ashley Carpenter on board.'

'Hmmm,' said Tudor. 'Put like that I concede it does sound pretty odd. You weren't selling this as a mystery cruise, were you? Or a celebrity whodunit?'

'It's not funny, dammit.'

She noticed that Tudor had suddenly stopped even pretending to pay attention to what she was saying but was focused uncompromisingly on the dance floor. The three-piece orchestra had switched to something Argentinian and tango-like. Surprisingly wild and raunchy. Gypsy music. The lead violin tossed her head and bared her teeth. The cellist and the pianist followed suit. Ambrose Perry and the others continued to shuffle, but a new and unexpected couple had taken to the floor and were executing what looked to Tudor's admittedly inexpert and untutored eye like a pretty passable piece of Latin-American exhibitionism. It was Dr Umlaut and Elizabeth Burney. Frau Umlaut did not look pleased.

'Good grief!' exclaimed Tudor. Little Miss Burney never ceased to surprise him. She was unrecognizable, all hips and slinkiness and as if she had a rose or carnation clutched between her canines. Something clenched between the buttocks too, he thought, and then checked himself. Little Umlaut wasn't bad either in a predictably mechanical parade-ground manner. He did the samba-rumba-tango or whatever, not like a Latin but in the manner of the Prussian Guard, as if taught by some Teutonic drill sergeant. The whole cabaret was a revelation. People noticed, even Ambrose Perry. Beside him Mandy Goldslinger gaped.

'Is that your little girl with that Kraut?'

'Elizabeth dancing with Dr Umlaut. Looks like it, yes.'

'If you call that dancing. Jeez. We don't get that kind of thing on the *Duchess* on the average cruise.'

Tudor gazed at the elderly stick-insects and mountainous jellies all around the pyrotechnical little German and his precocious Tasmanian sidekick and could see only too well that this must be true.

'We have to find Captain Sam,' said Tudor, bringing them both back to earth.

'Too right,' said Mandy.

'But it's sort of difficult to find someone if the powers-that-be deny that he's missing.'

'Can't we overrule Donaldson?'

'Not without Sam. Sam's the only man on board who out-ranks him. Sam can order him to do anything he likes but no one else can. Without Sam he is Sam, if you follow me.'

Tudor took a long draught of water and as if by magical osmosis Shane appeared with a chilly replacement. Tudor nodded gratefully and the maitre d' bared his fangs in acknowledgement.

'What you mean,' said Tudor, 'is that if Donaldson won't admit there's a problem we can't solve it.'

'You could put it like that.'

'Suppose I insist on seeing Sam.'

'You can insist as much as you like,' she said. 'I've tried that. He just says that Sam isn't well enough to see anyone, that he's sedated, that he can't speak because of the laryngitis and he specifically asked not to see anyone.'

'How could he do that if he's incapable of speech?'

'I imagine he wrote it down on a piece of paper. Sign language maybe. It doesn't matter. Angus Donaldson's word is law unless Sam is able to overrule him. And, what's more, can be seen to be able to overrule him.'

The three girls stopped playing their sexy foot-stamping number and acknowledged the applause of the tea-dancers and tea-drinkers. Some of the applause appeared to be aimed at Elizabeth and Dr Umlaut. Tea was now officially over. Drinking up time. Nothing to eat between now and olives and nuts in the happy hour which would begin in less than half an hour's time. There were plenty of passengers on board who browsed and sluiced on a non-stop basis. That's what they paid for.

Tudor pursed his lips.

'You're right,' he said, eventually, 'we've a lot of mysteries for just one little cruise. I'm not sure if they're connected or just coincidental. And I can't work out whether Captain Sam constitutes a mystery or just a straightforward medical indisposition.'

'The change of locks is a clincher, wouldn't you say?'

'I've only got your word for that,' he said.

'Are you calling me a liar?'

'Of course not. But. Well, there may be another explanation. A perfectly respectable one.'

'Nobody else knows about Sam and me,' she said.

'Don't be silly,' he said. 'I may not know this ship particularly well but one thing I do understand about closed societies such as this: you can't keep secrets. Everybody knows what everyone else is doing.'

'No one knows where Sam is. Or who changed the locks. Or why. Or about the gold. Or the lifeboat. Or the mysterious ships in mid-ocean. Life is suddenly nothing but secrets.'

'Not for long,' he said with certainty. 'I simply don't believe you can keep secrets on the *Duchess*. Not for any length of time.'

He looked up. Elizabeth was standing breathing heavily and perspiring gently. A bead of sweat stood out on her upper lip.

'Did I hear the word secret?' she said. 'I think you're right. Secrets will out. People can't keep them. Particularly during a *thé dansant* and revisiting the time of their life.'

Her two elders regarded her with a mixture of suspicion and admiration.

'Time to change for the next round,' she said. 'Dinner soon. Black tie evening.'

18

Tudor turned on the television in his cabin and was surprised to find a man talking about the Mutiny on the *Bounty*. He seemed quite articulate and to know about what he was talking. He did not look well, however, and was pale, if not exactly green about the gills. His tie was loosely tied, exposing the top button of his shirt. Occasionally he paused to take a sip of water from a glass on the table at his elbow.

It was a moment or two before Tudor realized that he was watching himself. He had been on the verge of saying that the lecturer was not nearly as good as *he* was. In fact, he was about to disagree with him about the 'inward happiness and peculiar pleasure' experienced by Captain Bligh when he was cast off the *Bounty* in the ship's boat. Would whoever was lowered over the side of the *Duchess* in the lifeboat have experienced similar emotions? 'Inward happiness and peculiar pleasure' were indeed the words that Bligh had written at the time in his running log. Whoever went off in the *Duchess*'s boat had kept no log.

Or if he had, it hadn't turned up.

He turned himself off. It was disconcerting to see himself in that way but at least the image was controllable. Good PR as well. He wondered how many others on board ship were dressing for dinner and watching his earlier performance. Freddie Grim? The Goronwy Watkyns? Prince Abdullah and his wives? The Umlauts? The Master? The Staff Captain? Mandy Goldslinger? Ambrose Perry and the gentlemen hosts? Who knew? He was tempted to ask 'Who cared?' But he knew that although he would never admit it to the world at large there was a part of him, probably a dominant part, that cared quite a lot. He craved an audience. Pity that he didn't come across better on TV.

There was a knock at the door and he abandoned his half-tied bow tie and went to open it. It was Elizabeth dressed to kill and for dinner. She was wearing the classic little black dress. It began late and finished early which, at *her* age and with *her* figure, was allowable. In a few years she'd have to start dressing a little more like mutton but for the time being she could do lamb and get away with it.

'Hi!' he said, non-committal as ever, and then, rather out of character, added, 'You're looking particularly nice.'

'Thanks,' she said, giving him a peck on the cheek. 'And you look a bit the worse for wear. Do you want me to tie your tie? Why don't you have a clip-on? Particularly when you so obviously can't tie your own. So how was La Goldslinger? What was so important?'

'I saw you with Umlaut. Dancing.'

'Of course.' She smelt nice as well as looking nice. Especially standing close behind him as she deftly fixed the tie around his neck. But she was about the same age as his daughter would have been if he had one. 'Nifty little mover our Walter.' She pronounced the name in an un-English way. 'Vultur'.

'Vultur,' he repeated, sounding idiotic.

'My new friend,' she said, pulling the black silk ends tight and straightening the tie in the glass. 'There,' she said, 'perfecto. Good enough to be fake. Yes, Dr Umlaut is Vultur and his wife is Irmgarde. They asked me to dinner in their suite. They have their own butler. I declined.'

'And Irmgarde doesn't mind you dancing with Vultur?'

'Not at all,' she smiled. 'It's good for him. He needs the exercise. He was the young foxtrot champion of Basel in his youth. She has a funny leg so she can't dance any more.

They used to be very good she says. So no. No objections.'

'Charming,' said Tudor, feeling his teeth gritting. 'So Basel. Swiss not Kraut?'

'*Schwitzer-kraut*,' she said. 'Pharmaceuticals. Umlaut, Umlaut and Umlaut. Or something like that. His great grandfather invented the oral contraceptive. At least I think that's what he meant. He was a bit coy about it. So what's your news? What did La Goldslinger want? Don't tell me, it was a proposition: she wants to get you into bed.'

He turned round and took his jacket off its hanger. He was wearing braces, plain dark-blue ones with gold-coloured clips; his shoes had toe-caps and laces and were highly polished. He was that sort of man. Dull, he thought to himself. When all was said and done he was dull. He so very much wished not to be and made every effort to be interesting. But deep down he knew that he wasn't. Elizabeth on the other hand was. It was annoying. Very.

'No Madam Goldslinger did not make a pass.' He shrugged into his dinner jacket and patted non-existent dandruff off the shoulders.

'Snap then,' she said. 'Vultur didn't make a pass at me either. Though I wouldn't put it past them at dinner. I have a feeling they're a kinky couple. I suspect she likes to watch. Only guessing but there's something about them that's kind of fishy. In a sexual way. Know what I mean? Anyway, tell me: what *did* la Goldslinger want?'

He patted his pockets to make sure he had keys, wallet and a handkerchief.

'She's been having an affair with the Captain. With Sam Hardy.'

'Yes,' she said. 'I thought you knew that.'

He looked at her sharply. 'Did you know?'

'Everybody knew.'

'Mandy thought it was a secret.'

'Oh,' she shrugged, 'people who are having illicit affairs always assume they've managed to keep their guilty secret when they've failed to do so. You know that.'

'I suppose.' It was years since Tudor had enjoyed an illicit affair or even harboured a guilty secret. His professional studies told him that what the girl said was true but he knew it only in a professional academic sense. Vicarious, not visceral. It was at moments like this that he wondered if his copper friends such as Chief Inspector Trythall back home at the Wessex Constabulary didn't have a point. Trythall's approach to crime was sharp-end stuff. His was ivory-tower. It was a point Trythall enjoyed making. He himself countered by arguing that a certain dispassionate, cool academic examination was more valuable than gut reactions. But, privately, he had doubts. At moments such as this he wondered if he were too thin-blooded.

'People like Mandy Goldslinger never seem to understand how visible they are. She's a celebrity on board ship. Likewise old Popeye Sam Hardy. She can't sneeze without the passengers and crew catching a cold. Nor he.'

She sat down on Tudor's bed and yawned.

'Been quite a day,' she said, 'I hadn't imagined cruising would be so exciting. So Mandy let you into a secret that the rest of them have been sharing for as long as the relationship's been going on. Then what? I got something useful out of Vultur so you'd better have something other than *l'affaire* Hardy-Goldslinger. Sounds like a new ship's cocktail — a local take on the Harvey Wallbanger.'

'The Harvey Wallbanger was invented by Duke Antone in the 1950s,' said Tudor. 'A local surfer called Harvey had a bad day on the beach and consoled himself in the Blackwatch Bar run by Antone with rather too many of the Duke's special Screwdrivers which were vodka and orange with a dash of Galliano. When he got up to go he couldn't find the door and kept bumping into walls. Hence Harvey Wallbanger.'

191

'I'm impressed,' said Elizabeth stifling a second yawn, 'so what else did Mandy tell you?'

'That she's lost her lover. She can't find Sam any more than anyone else. But what's really sinister is that they've changed the locks on his cabin door. Mandy had a set of keys but now she can't get in.'

'So who's 'they'?'

'I don't know. Angus Donaldson's in charge if Sam's not with us. He gives the orders, has the authority. If someone else changed the locks Angus would have the right to overrule them.'

'So why would Donaldson change the locks?'

'So that people like Mandy couldn't get into the captain's cabin.'

'And why would he want to do that?'

'Because the cabin contains something that he doesn't want Mandy to find.'

She frowned. 'Or nothing,' she said.

'How do you mean?'

'It's like the dog in the night,' she said. 'Not the barking but the lack of barking. The conceit is that Captain Sam is lying in his own bed speechless on account of his laryngitis. But suppose he's been bumped off and tipped overboard, then there's no one in the Captain's cabin and the emptiness has to

192

be concealed from prying eyes.'

'So,' said Tudor, aware that he was not functioning at the top of his range, 'Angus Donaldson is responsible for the murder of Captain Sam and is covering up by having the locks changed, shutting the cabin up and keeping the keys.'

'It's a theory,' said Elizabeth. 'Perfectly plausible. Except that in a few days we'll be docking and the NYPD will be all over the *Duchess* like marauding ants.'

'So he's got till then to work out a final solution.'

'Yup,' said the girl, tossing her head. 'I guess you're right. Nothing else you have to tell me?'

'No,' he said, sitting down heavily in one of his two status-conferring armchairs, 'Your turn now. Go ahead. Shoot.'

'Well,' she said, giving the impression of a story-teller who is anxious to make the most of a good, if tall tale, 'you've noticed that the Umlauts and Prince Abdullah aren't exactly the best of pals.'

'It hadn't escaped my notice,' said Tudor drily. 'But you wouldn't expect it? They both behave as if they owned the ship. Naturally they can't stand the sight of each other. It's alpha-male stuff. Testosterone. Everything is part of the game. Take the wives. Parading

193

them around the ship is the sheikh's way of putting two fingers up at Walter. Poor old Walter's only got Irmgarde. Or did, until you came along and inveigled him on to the dance floor.'

She turned mildly pink.

'It's one way to get the little man to spill beans,' she said. 'Anyway who said Prince Abdullah was a sheikh?'

'You know what I mean,' said Tudor. 'Personally I have a feeling he's a phoney so it doesn't much matter whether he's a fake-sheikh or a fake-prince. It's the fakery that's significant, not the title to which he's pretending.'

'Hmmm,' said Elizabeth. 'I don't know about Middle-Eastern titles but I think the money's real. He's loaded. So is Herr Doktor Umlaut.'

'OK,' said Tudor, 'they're both rich as Croesus and Umlaut's ancestor made a fortune out of oral contraceptives. What else did he tell you?'

'Guess,' she said.

'Oh, for heaven's sake. I'm not in the mood. He's challenging Prince Abdullah to a duel. Pistols at dawn.'

'Many a true word,' she said. 'It's not a duel in that sense but it is a kind of *mano-a-mano* deal. Kids in the playground stuff. Umlaut wants to buy the ship.'

'And so does the Prince.'

'Right on,' she said. 'They both want it and the board is split. There's an Umlaut faction and a Prince Abdullah faction. What's more, the split extends beyond the boardroom. Sam Hardy is the on-board rep of one of the factions and Angus Donaldson of the other. Umlaut is a Donaldson man; the Prince is a Sam supporter. Neither of them will stop at anything.'

'So.' Tudor looked at his watch and wondered if they should venture back into what for the moment passed as the outside world and prepare themselves for the next round of gourmandizing. 'Both these shady plutocrats want to buy the ship. Whichever one succeeds will effectively bar the van-quished one from ever setting foot on board again.'

'*Ja-wohl* as Vultur would say.'

'And are you telling me that your little Basel billionaire might have bumped off Captain Sam?'

She looked thoughtful. 'I'm not saying he did,' she said eventually, 'and I'm not saying he didn't. But he had at least half a motive and he's more than unscrupulous enough. It's a chance.'

'Interesting,' he said. 'It hadn't occurred to

me that the rivalry was quite so intense.'

'No,' she agreed, 'me neither. Whose side are you on?'

'We don't take sides,' he said. 'You know that.'

19

The bar outside the entrance to the Chatsworth restaurant was called the Mitford, a little act of homage to one of the best known Devonshire Duchesses — Debo, youngest of the famous Mitford sisters. A portrait of her hung in a prominent position alongside photographs of herself and her sisters, including Nancy, the novelist, Diana, the wife of Sir Oswald Moseley, Unity, the friend of the Führer who shot herself in a park in Munich, and the radical Jessica who settled in the United States and wrote a best-seller about American funeral customs.

Riviera Shipping's design department had done a sparky job on the bar which exuded exactly the sort of brittle period charm Tudor associated with the Mitford girls. It was almost decadent but in a chintzy chocolate box way that saved it from being dangerous. Just right for a cruise liner. No threat.

All tables were taken so Tudor and Elizabeth sat on bar stools and picked abstractedly at olives, Twiglets and tiny cheese biscuits presented in small silvery bowls of the sort you might expect a Mitford girl to encounter in a Grand Hotel. Sitting on bar stools made one susceptible to interruption and so it proved. The interloper, in a white tuxedo of the sort one would expect to see at a sub-standard award ceremony involving C-list celebrities, was Ambrose Perry, gentleman host. He was, briefly, unattached.

'Formidable tango,' he said, easing himself on to the stool next to Elizabeth, 'Where did you learn?'

'Tasmania,' said Elizabeth. 'I did a dance minor at uni. We had an exiled Chilean poet who'd been a senior diplomat under Allende. Should have seen his fandango. Cool.'

'I thought you were remarkable. I myself have earned a modest crust from ballroom exertions of one sort or another and I know enough to recognize quality. Accept, please, my felicitations.'

'Will you have a drink?' asked Tudor, who had already ordered a couple of Harvey Wallbangers in acknowledgement of their earlier conversation. Perry said he wouldn't mind if he did and his was a white wine spritzer.

'Enjoying your cruise?' he asked conversationally and, apparently, innocently.

'Yes,' said Elizabeth. 'She's a great ship. Food and drink's excellent. Company ditto. What more could a girl want?'

'You should have seen the *France*,' said Ambrose. 'She was the ultimate. The acme. Never been a ship like her.'

Elizabeth nibbled a pretzel.

'She must have been amazing,' she said. 'But I like the *Duchess*. She's cute.'

'The *France* was never cute,' said Perry. He had a face like a lizard. All wrinkle. The eyes were slits and you half-expected a forked tongue to flick out from behind the pursed lips and spear an olive from the silver bowl. Or maybe an errant insect if one should fly within range. He could be any age but even if he wasn't he seemed ancient. 'I'm not sure the *Duchess* is cute either, but the *France* had a touch of class. More than a touch. She was class through and through.'

He sipped at his spritzer and patted his mouth with a linen napkin immediately afterwards, removing the salty aftermath of a peanut. He was fastidious — fussily so.

'I'm glad you're enjoying the trip,' said Elizabeth, unconvincingly.

'I didn't say I was enjoying it,' said the host. His fastidiousness clearly extended to speech and judgement as well as dress and manners. 'Gentlemanly hosting is a job. Enjoyment would be an inappropriate response. Satisfaction maybe, but enjoyment, no. It would be like having fun. My job is to enable others to have fun not for me to have fun myself.'

'Oh,' said Elizabeth feeling, rightly, that she had been put in her place.

'And are your old ladies enjoying themselves?' asked Tudor, sensing that this was the question Ambrose Perry was waiting for.

'I believe so,' he said, appearing to think quite hard about what was the correct answer, 'The ship-board activities are exemplary as they always are. The little girls from Latvia play prettily and, as you know, with *brio* when it is appropriate. The bingo is well called. The bridge is popular and the pairs well-matched. Few play chess but boards and pieces are there as always and one or two of us if not in quite the Grandmaster class are always ready to oblige. The jigsaws are stimulating. The library well stocked. Fruit machines are not to my taste nor to that of the majority of my ladies. The food and drink throughout are delicious. With all this I find no fault.'

Both Tudor and Elizabeth could sense a big 'but' looming.

Elizabeth anticipated it.

'But,' she said helpfully.

Ambrose did not look like a man who wanted help. Particularly from a woman. At least not from a young woman. It occurred to both Elizabeth and Tudor that when it came

200

to women Ambrose was like a conservative oenophile. He liked only old vintages. Anything *spritzig* made him nervous. Beaujolais Nouveau upset him. Younger elements would say that he only liked women when they were past their sell-by date. It was not that he didn't like women. He would not have been doing the job that he did if he didn't. But he only really liked old ducks. He was a sexually inverted snob — unimpressed by nubility.

'But nothing,' he said, sipping another sip of spritzer and nibbling a nut. 'However, there is, how shall I put this? There is a *mood*.' He pronounced the word as if it were the noise a cow might make, giving it an extra syllable or two, as if building an extra section into its middle.

'A mood,' repeated Tudor. 'How do you mean, 'mood'? Bad mood, good mood, foul mood, moody mood.' Drink and fatigue were making him facetious. Elizabeth dug a pointy toe into his shin.

'I'm not entirely sure I'd qualify the mood one way or another,' said Ambrose, 'but I definitely detect one. You could call it an atmosphere if you preferred. It might perhaps be one of anticipation. Or merely heightened awareness. It may, of course, pass. But' — and he speared an olive and regarded it thoughtfully before popping it between his overly regular dentures — 'there again, it may not.'

Tudor and Elizabeth were not entirely sure what he was talking about but judged it better not to admit it. Better to say nothing. Thus encouraged he might expand and become more intelligible. They both therefore had another sip and another olive.

Presently, Perry said, 'Mrs Potts, for example. Olive. With whom I was sharing the floor earlier. She senses a mood too.'

'Can you be more specific?' asked Tudor, not sure whether Olive Potts' analysis of mood or atmosphere was worth knowing. Or that of Ambrose Perry come to that. Still, it was better, surely, to know what people were talking about than to be left stumbling through a fog of ambiguity.

'This morning's business,' said Perry, 'is a case in point. One minute, confusion, strange voices on the public address system, clear indications of something amiss. Then suddenly and for no apparent reason, all is suddenly well again. The ship continues on its way as if nothing has happened. In Olive Potts' eyes that creates uncertainty. An unsettled atmosphere. A bad mood.'

'I thought,' said Tudor, deliberately disingenuously, 'that this morning's stuff was some sort of anti-terrorist exercise. I'm afraid I didn't take it terribly seriously. I assumed it was a sort of Bush-Blair inspired equivalent of lifeboat drill. If it isn't Health and Safety Regulations it's the War on Terror. Even on board ship.'

'That's what you were lecturing on, surely,' said Perry. 'Captain Bligh and the *Bounty* was the eighteenth-century equivalent of what we're experiencing today. Fletcher Christian was the contemporary equivalent of a suicide bomber. Captain Bligh was in charge of Neighbourhood Watch.'

'I didn't see you at the talk,' said Tudor supiciously.

'No,' said Perry, 'I watched you on TV when I was preparing for dinner. Very good if I may say so, but not necessarily conducive to improving the mood. A little like showing the film *Titanic* as a matinée on board.'

'Well,' said Tudor, 'I wouldn't go as far as that. You wouldn't get the Mutiny on the *Bounty* happening in this day and age. We've become far too sophisticated.'

Ambrose Perry rolled a nut round his mouth and seemed on the verge of spitting it out but evidently thought better of it and chewed and swallowed instead.

'I'm delighted to hear you say so,' he said. 'But I have to say that the Master's laryngitis is disturbing some of my elderly friends. Mrs Dolly Mather-Jenkins from New Jersey for instance. She is of a naturally nervous disposition, but she is concerned at the Master's silence. Even if he can't speak one might hope that he would come among us if only to be hail fellow and well met in silence.'

'I understand he's not at all well,' said Elizabeth. 'Doctor says he must get some rest.'

Tudor glanced at her and wondered if he should kick her shins too. Why were they both telling porkies?

'I'm sorry to hear it,' said Ambrose. 'I've always had a softish spot for Master Sam whereas there is something not entirely to my taste when it comes to the Scottish Staff Captain. My ladies, I have to report, are of a similar mind.'

'I'm sorry to hear it,' said Tudor. 'But I hope you'll allay their fears. I'm sure you will. I can't think of more capable hands for them to be in.'

He drained his glass and smiled at Elizabeth.

'I think it's time we went in, don't you?'

'I'm really not terribly hungry,' she said. 'I think I'll just stick to a couple of ounces of Beluga and a lightly seared *filet*. Or maybe a tuna steak.'

Tudor got off his stool and stood aside.

'A *bientôt*,' he said pleasantly to the gentleman host who smiled not altogether agreeably and raised his glass at their retreating forms.

'Rum cove,' said Tudor, as they paused to wash their hands in the new regulation sani-fluid at the door of the Chatsworth restaurant.

'Rum's the word,' said Elizabeth, raising her eyebrows.

It was too. There was rum everywhere. Or a mixture of rum and brandy and Grand Marnier depending on whether one was having babas or crêpes Suzettes or steak Dianes or dinde Duchesse or choufleur Chatsworth or moules Mitfords. Rum or not, strong spirits were everywhere leaping towards the low ceiling as men in striped trousers and jet black jackets set fire to food of every description after smothering it in alcohol. The room was like a veritable Hell's Kitchen — Hieronymus Bosch meets the *Sunday Times* Colour Supplement: Delia with Danger.

The two of them threaded their way gingerly past the various table-side conflagrations nodding in a correctly friendly way to the Umlauts, Prince Abdullah and wives, the Grims, the Goronwy Watkyns and various other old or new acquaintances.

Their stewardess, Helga, brought iced water and menus to their now familiar table.

'Neither of us is terribly hungry, I'm afraid,' said Tudor. They both smiled ingratiatingly.

'How about a little Beluga, followed by a rare steak with spinach?' asked Helga in flawless English. She had been here before. 'And shall I send Igor?'

Igor was the sommelier with a superior jacket and a tastevin suspended from his neck. He'd know that because Tudor was paying for the wine he would have a cheap bottle. That meant he would not rate special glasses, or indeed, much in the way of special attention either.

Tudor gazed around the Chatsworth and smiled.

'You wouldn't get away with this on dry land,' he said. 'In fact I'm quite surprised they get away with it in mid-Atlantic. There must be international safety regulations which tell you how high flames are allowed to go in the dining-room. I'm surprised they're allowed flames at all. Read, mark etcetera etcetera for you will not see the like again. At least not anywhere with an ounce of political correctness.'

The two of them gazed around this

anachronistic temple of 1950s cooking at the table.

'Restaurants were like this once,' said Tudor, 'before you were born. In the days when Sir Bernard and Lady Docker were the stuff of the William Hickey Column in the *Daily Express* and all was right with the world. That was before huge salaries for footballers and commodity brokers, when the workers wore clogs and the Trades Unions — '

He didn't finish the sentence for a few tables away there was an uncontrolled explosion, a whoosh of flame greater even than that which was usual for the Chatsworth room and a plume of smoke which suggested that one of the penguin-outfitted maitre d's had made a dreadful mistake.

'Bomb,' said Elizabeth. 'Bombe Surprise!'

20

She was right. It was a big bang.

Tudor swore.

'That wasn't a gastro-explosion,' he said, 'that was the real thing. An Ambrose Perry. His old ladies are going to be in a serious mood now.'

The way in which the Chatsworth staff transformed themselves from food and drink flunkeys to para-medics was impressive. Tudor was reminded of military bandsmen who, in time of war, doubled up as stretcher-bearers.

In fact stretchers were called to the table in a far corner of the room though from what Tudor and Elizabeth could see there was no great need for them. The people who were being stretchered off were walking wounded. They must have been shocked and they would surely have suffered a degree of burning, but they were not dead and they did not appear to have been seriously injured. It looked from a distance as if there were two guests on the casualty list and perhaps a couple of members of staff. The silence which had descended upon the room lifted as abruptly as it had fallen. It was replaced by a buzz of conversation several decibels higher than the muted level of what had gone before.

Suddenly waiters emerged through the swing doors to the galley carrying trays on which there were enough filled brandy balloons to provide each diner with a glass. Classic treatment for shock. Nothing was said. It was all done crisply, efficiently and with a uniformly stiff upper lip.

'Well,' said Elizabeth, accepting the proffered medicine, 'quite a day. And I thought cruising was an escape and a relaxation. Silly me!'

'Oh, I think appearances are deceptive,' said Tudor. 'It's like effortless superiority. The more effortless it appears the more effort has actually gone into it. Same on board ship. The smoother and more relaxed everything seems to be the more blood, sweat and tears it has actually cost.'

'You reckon?'

'I reckon,' he said. 'I also have a sense that whatever it was may have been aimed at your new friends Herr Doctor and Frau Umlaut. Weren't they sitting over there?'

They both peered in the direction of the pall of smoke which hung blue and acrid over what little remained of the dining table in the far corner. Someone had moved swiftly with a fire extinguisher so there was a lot of foam about. Also charred table and cloth. Essentially, however, it seemed that damage was minimal. The shock was considerable; the explosion spectacular; the consequences depressing but the short-term effects nothing much.

And so to caviar and steak and a Chilean Merlot. The sang-froid was so thick you could have cut it with a standard-issue butter knife let alone one of the sabre-toothed specialist jobs which came with the *filet*. But this was a British ship and although her Britishness had been diluted her *esprit* was undimmed. Rule Britannia and all that. Britons never ever would be slaves. And all that as well.

'A murder attempt that failed?' asked Tudor, 'Or a signally successful warning? It's one or the other.'

'Conspiracy or cock-up,' said Elizabeth. She ordered her caviar straight without egg, onions or sour cream. Ever the purist.

'If the victims were the Umlauts, the greatest enemy they have on board is Prince Abdullah. Do you think he's trying to kill them?'

'It's so easy,' she said, 'someone just has to drop some paraffin on to the steak Diane or whatever, just before the waiter lights his match and *pouf!* you've singed the King of Spain's beard. In a manner of speaking. If you see what I mean.'

'And anyone can have done it?'

She shrugged. 'If that's what it was. After all, you can apparently blow up a Boeing with a mixture of Vodka, lemonade and toothpaste so it really wouldn't be too difficult to lethalize a flambéed steak or crêpe. Simplicity itself. Do you imagine the powers-that-be will slap a ban on table-side cooking? I would. Remember your friend *Tipperary Tatler* is on the loose. Perhaps it's her doing.'

They both stared ruminatively into space and wondered how long it would be before an element of panic was introduced to the ship. Once that happened it would spread as rapidly and inexorably as germs in the air-conditioning or a dreaded lurgy in the galley.

'Gosh,' said Tudor, snapping out of his reverie. 'What's this?' Between his knife and fork there now rested a piece of stiff creamy card with the ship's crest on it and his name printed in crude black ink capital letters. DOCTOR TUDOR CORNWALL. He stared at it suspiciously and then turned it over. On the other side was a message.

'MYOB,' he read. 'Or you're next. And you'll be all fire and no smoke.'

'MYOB?' queried Elizabeth.

'An acronym for Mind Your Own Business,'

said Tudor. 'Haven't heard that since, oh, university I suppose. It was a catch-phrase of Ashley Carpenter as a matter of fact.'

'I never heard him use it.' Elizabeth had been Carpenter's pupil in the not-so-distant bad old days. Her relationship had been more than academic so she should have known about his own business.

'You came after that time,' said Tudor. 'He would have adopted a new range of acronyms and acrostics by your day. Or abandoned them altogether. Always up with the latest fashion was our Ashley.'

'Do you think' — Elizabeth looked implausibly ingenuous — 'that MYOB is a signal that he's on board and pulling strings? Seems a strange message otherwise.'

Caviar came. The helping seemed larger even than usual. If it were true that an army marched on its stomach it was even more true, thought Tudor, of a cruise liner full of paying passengers. Give the punters too much to eat and they'll be lulled into a false sense of security before you can say knife.

'There's no way that Ashley Carpenter can be on board the *Duchess*,' said Tudor. 'I mean, we'd know.'

'Not necessarily,' said Elizabeth. 'He's a terrible tease.'

'He didn't get on in the UK,' said Tudor,

'and I'm pretty sure he didn't embark in Cobh.'

'Maybe,' said Elizabeth, 'he came in the other night. Off the Irish lectureboat. Swapped places with the Captain.'

Tudor rubbed his chin and ate a mother-of-pearl spoonful of Beluga. They did things properly in the Chatsworth.

'Why would he do that?'

'No telling with Ashley,' she said. 'He hates you, that's obvious, and he's keen to get back at me for some reason. Also he has increasing tendencies to megalomania. I don't see any reason for not thinking that he's up to his ears with this gang of hijackers wherever they come from and whoever they are. He's quite doolally.'

'First of all the Irish press party or whoever they are stage a ham-fisted attempt to hijack the ship,' he said. 'They fail but *Tipperary Tatler* escapes and is still at large.'

'Possibly attempting to incinerate the Umlauts.'

'Precisely,' said Tudor, 'and, for the sake of an alternative theory, warning me off with anonymous notes.'

'OK.' The girl shovelled Beluga into her mouth. She clearly found the dainty spoon too mimsy. Caviar wasn't meant to be nibbled, not where she came from.

'Do we think that Ashley and *Tipperary Tatler* are in cahoots?'

'I don't know,' said Elizabeth. 'Ashley was always attracted to dangerous Bohemian redheads. And I think because he sees himself as a failure in conventional terms he wants to remedy the situation with the most radical solution he can find. In other words, violence. He wants to shoot his way into *Who's Who*. The only way he can even manage a footnote in history is by bombing his way in. He's the John Wilkes Booth of our times. He can't be a great man himself so he'll kill one to secure a vicarious destiny. Greatness by proxy. What do you think? You were his contemporary.'

This was true. Tudor and Ashley had competed for the same girl; argued at the same tutorials; got drunk together; played squash against each other; rowed briefly in the same eight; drank beer and sometimes Scotch in each other's company; lied on each other's behalf. Been friends. Now, for reasons that Tudor still found difficult to clearly comprehend they had become the best of enemies. It was something to do with jealousy, though quite what he was not entirely sure. Ashley seemed to him, as he always had done, at least as much a suitable subject for envy himself.

He had no inkling of this enmity until

Ashley had invited him down under as a visiting fellow and plotted against him in a cunning and almost lethal way. One legacy of that bizarre encounter was Elizabeth Burney who had once been Ashley's own star pupil and also much much more. Now she was his though only in an academic and never in a million years a carnal one. He had hoped that Ashley would vanish but like the proverbial bad penny he kept turning up when least expected or wanted. The girl and he had privately christened him a latter day Moriarty to Tudor's Holmes. Now here he was once more. Apparently. Perhaps.

Now Mandy Goldslinger also turned up, breathing heavily, flushed, flustered and wearing a little black dress which, as is the way with little black dresses, particularly when worn by ladies of a certain age and a particular disposition began too early and finished too late. Or something like that. It certainly seemed to Tudor that there was not enough of it.

La Goldslinger's impressive breast was heaving with a combination of over-exertion and over-emotion. She appeared to have been running in a literal and metaphorical top gear. And quite possibly been at the brandy.

'There's someone in the Captain's cabin,' she said, breathlessly.

'Someone?' Tudor was intrigued. 'You mean someone other than a skipper stricken by laryngitis?'

'If it's Sam he wouldn't submit to house arrest. I don't think Sam's on board, wherever he is. I think there's someone else in there.'

Elizabeth and Tudor looked at each other meaningfully. They were both thinking Ashley Carpenter. Neither said anything. Professor Carpenter was unlikely to mean anything to Mandy Goldslinger.

'How do you know?' asked Elizabeth.

'A tray,' said the Cruise Director. 'I saw someone with a tray with dinner on it. They knocked on the door and it was opened from inside. The girl went in.'

'Girl?'

'Yes. A stewardess. In *Duchess* uniform.'

'Did you notice anything about her particularly?' Tudor wanted to know but he could tell from her expression that Mandy couldn't tell one member of crew from another. Or didn't. They were like servants to a feudal aristocrat. They all looked the same and were, basically, beneath notice. They merely fetched and carried. A bartender on board mixed cocktails. Why would one know his name or face?

'She was just one of those girls.'

'*Tipperary Tatler*,' said Elizabeth in a 'Eureka! I've got it' tone of voice which owed more to intuition than forensics. There was no reason on earth for thinking that the captain's cabin girl was the Irish terrorist. Elizabeth was playing a hunch. She was good at it, but Chief Inspector Trythall would not have approved. No method, he would have said — typical girl. He, like any good copper, marched inexorably through the alphabet taking in every letter as he went. Not for him these sudden inspired leaps from A to Z.

Mandy Goldslinger looked at her as if she were mad.

'The Irish terrorist girl who escaped,' said Tudor helpfully. 'She originally claimed to work for this fictitious magazine so we've named her after it. Sorry!'

La Goldslinger gave the lady Cruise Director's equivalent of a snort, managing with a gesture and something between a sniff and a sneeze, that she just hated having to deal on equal terms with delinquent children.

'I don't see that the identity of the serving girl is relevant,' she said, sounding like Queen Elizabeth I reprimanding an over-familiar courtier, 'the point is, surely, that the Captain's cabin is occupied.'

'And you previously thought it was empty?'

'Well, yes. Maybe. What do you think's

happened to Sam? Has he been murdered?'

'You could take things at face value,' said Tudor, not believing himself or even convinced that he was saying what he heard, 'that poor old Sam's got laryngitis, doesn't want to be disturbed and has lost his voice.'

'The day old Sam loses his voice,' boomed a familiar Celtic foghorn, 'is the day I have it off with the Pope. My view is that old Sam's finally done a runner. Jumped ship and taken the crown jewels with him. He always was a shifty old bugger.'

Mandy Goldslinger began to cry.

21

It was indeed Walter and Irmgarde Umlaut who had suffered incendiary indignity in the Chatsworth that night. Their wounds were, however, more cosmetic than damaging. What's more the Umlauts were very cross. Vultur, in particular, was incandescent.

You had to hand it to them, thought Tudor, they were back in the Chatsworth in time for a brace of champagne sorbets and a couple of double espressos. Regular undaunted Prussian Guards, they didn't frighten easily. Blackened but unbowed.

Sir Goronwy and Lady Watkyn passed unsteadily by their table and paused. 'I'm giving them the Porthole Murder tomorrow,' said the bardic Watkyn portentously. 'Steady the Buffs and all that. Not too near the bone, I hope.'

'You mean Gay Gibson, James Camb, the *Durban Castle*, Khaki Roberts and all that?'

'I didn't know it was a speciality of yours,' said the Welshman.

'It isn't,' said Tudor. 'I've read Herbstein's book that's all.'

'Ah.' Sir Goronwy's eyes were rheumy and

his expression sceptical, 'Port holes, missing persons, illicit sex . . . recurring perils of life at sea.'

Mandy Goldslinger sniffed tearfully.

'I have great faith in the Celtic tendency,' said Sir Goronwy. 'The Welsh and the Scots will see us through.'

'But not, I think, the Irish,' said Tudor meaningfully.

'Perhaps not,' said Watkyn. 'On which note I'll bid you *adieu*.'

'Pompous git,' said Elizabeth.

'What was all that about the Port hole case?' asked Mandy, still lachrymose.

'A stewardess on a ship called the *Durban Castle* vanished one night. She was pushed through a port hole by a man called Camb who got off on a technicality. Well, wasn't hanged. He did a long stretch in Dartmoor. Sex that went wrong is what it looks like. Happens quite often on ocean liners. They seem to be havens of innocence and safety but in reality they're hotbeds of lust, crime and sudden death. Like the benign, smiling English countryside. Like the *Duchess*.'

A sombre silence ensued.

'We have a missing captain which may have a perfectly innocent explanation,' said Elizabeth, 'and an attempted hijack which may have been a silly student prank. And a lifeboat loaded with gold ingots which was returned intact. So, *ipso facto*, no provable crime has been committed.'

'That's one interpretation,' said Tudor, 'but the other is that we have a murder or abduction, attempted theft on an extremely ambitious scale and a thwarted act of piracy on the high seas.'

'None of which you can prove.'

Caviar plates were cleared. Steak came.

'You don't like Donaldson,' said Tudor, addressing Mandy Goldslinger.

'Of course not,' she said. 'Why should I? He's been after Sam's job for years but he's not up to it. And he disapproves of the relationship between the two of us.'

'So he knows.'

'He's never said anything outright but he knows. Or at least suspects. He and Sam work in the same office. If you see what I mean. And Angus isn't stupid.'

'But straight.'

'No reason to think otherwise,' she said. 'Like I said, I don't care for him, but I can't pin a dishonesty rap on him. He's always acted by the book.'

'And where does he fit in the present scheme?' asked Tudor. 'Sam is out of it. Whether it's just laryngitis or something more serious is irrelevant. I hate to seem insensitive but that's the way it is. Angus is the man we have to deal with whether we like it or not.'

Mandy sighed. 'Angus sails the ship,' she said. 'That's his job. That's his expertise. Sam is front of house. Sam is the image. He's what the punters enjoy; what they trust; why they sign up for the *Duchess*; why they love Riviera Shipping.'

'But Sam's the boss,' said Elizabeth. 'Angus has to defer if they disagree.'

'They don't disagree,' said Mandy, 'not openly. They can't. Their duties just don't overlap. It's like Sam's front of house and Angus is the chef.'

'That's the theory,' said Tudor. 'What about the reality?'

'What you see is what you get.' The Cruise Director seemed surprised. A lifetime of selling illusion might have robbed her of the ability to distinguish between fact and fiction, thought Tudor. She couldn't do her job if, to an extent, she didn't believe her own publicity. That made her an unreliable witness. On the other hand she was the only member of staff in whom he could really trust. Or could he? So many grey areas. It made life unsettling but it was the nature of the job. Criminal affairs did not concern certainties. Post-mortems reflected the mortems themselves: grey, shadowy, murky, always open to doubt and debate. It was part of what made crime so fascinating.

'You're telling me that Angus and Sam were — are — peas in a pod?' asked Tudor.

'Of course not,' said Mandy Goldslinger, with something approaching asperity. Except that Cruise Directors didn't do asperity. They did schmooze and spin.

'You mean they told one story and lived another,' said Tudor.

'No.' She was irritated now, even though she knew that Tudor was a necessary ally. 'They lived the same story and told the same story. They were both reading from the same hymn sheet. There's no argument. They were a team — whatever they may have felt privately.'

Silence ensued. The atmosphere in the Chatsworth was edgy. It would have been extraordinary if it had been anything else. Atmospheres were elusive concepts. Tudor and Trythall argued about them incessantly. Trythall and other police procedurals denied their existence and believed that even if they did exist they were irrelevant to what actually happened. The presence of the seriously singed Umlauts didn't help any more than the obvious truculence of those at Prince Abdullah's table, leering across the room. There was an atmosphere and you could cut it with the proverbial knife.

'I don't like it,' said Elizabeth. 'I'm getting bad vibes.'

'Relax,' said Mandy Goldslinger, 'everything's under control.' She wasn't convincing, didn't sound as if she meant it. The little tub in the middle of the vasty deep suddenly seemed a terribly vulnerable place to be.

'I need to talk to Donaldson,' said Tudor. 'He's in charge whether we like it or not.'

'You,' said Elizabeth, 'have no standing in any of this. Goronwy Watkyn and Freddie Grim are just as well qualified. In any case, Angus Donaldson simply has to take us to our destination and the American authorities will sort everything out. So relax. Go with the flow.'

'I disagree,' said Tudor. 'I don't think the American authorities *will* sort it out. My sense is that they still have a blind spot when it comes to Irish republicans, and Irish republicans are one of the threads we're contending with here. I think the American process is even more susceptible to hot-shot lawyers than the British one. I think they'll be out of sympathy and kilter with what is still, despite the Prince and the Umlauts, a British-owned shipping line. So actually my view is that American so-called justice will screw up and we'd be much better solving the whole thing at sea before we dock.'

'You sound like a crusty old xenophobe,' Elizabeth laughed scornfully. 'I thought you were better than that.'

'Tudor may be right,' said Mandy Goldslinger unexpectedly. 'I'm not too happy about the idea of the NYPD followed by the course of American justice. I can see our poor little ship being impounded for months if not years while nothing much happens at vast expense.'

'And Mandy's American,' said Tudor with a self-satisfaction bordering on triumphalism.

'If you're determined to try to solve it single-handed without benefit of due legal and forensic process then I think you have to see Angus Donaldson and have a serious discussion with him.' Elizabeth was being uncharacteristically sensible, even pedantic. 'In Sam's absence Donaldson's in charge. You simply have to get his clearance. As we've said there's already a sort of official ship's system for sorting out misdemeanours at sea even if it's only a semi-competent Master-at-Arms and his minions. You've also got Freddie Grim and Goronwy Watkyn, both of whom think their credentials are as good as yours. Or better.'

She was right. They all knew it.

'No time like the present,' he said, smiling

225

at Mandy. 'Can you fix?'

'Sure,' she said. 'Angus and I have very correct and cordial relations. There'll be no problems.'

She stood and left. Tudor sighed and gazed round the emptying restaurant. Staff were stacking, polishing glasses, laying tables for next morning's breakfast. Passengers had mostly left heading for the cinema or the ballroom where the evening entertainment of crooner, crooneuse, stand-up comedian and the ship's dancers, mainly classically trained Romanians would have to be introduced in just under ten minutes. A job for La Goldslinger though she might have delegated it to one of her two assistants in view of the pressing matter of pinning down the Staff Captain.

The ship lunged lightly, reminding them, as she did from time to time, that she was a ship and not a grand hotel. It was such a strange phenomenon, this salty escape which was in its way a self-imposed imprisonment. Hell was gentlemen hosts, he mused. Or other passengers. Or nothing to do but eat and drink and be fried lobster-pink by sun, sea and wind. After a day or so it took him ten minutes to decide whether to have a gin and tonic or a Tom Collins.

'May we join you?'

It was Vultur and Irmgarde, fresh from bonfire night.

They were both clutching coffee cups and liqueur glasses and looking blackened but unbowed.

'I apologize,' said Doctor Umlaut, 'for the earlier diversion. It must have been upsetting for everybody.'

'Not as much as for you,' said Tudor politely.

'It is nothing,' he said, as they sat down heavily. Tudor and Elizabeth's table was a four, laid for two, but with a quartet of chairs, 'but whether a mistake or something more sinister, well . . . ' He grinned. 'Occasionally I feel times at sea are in need of a little enlivening. Storm perhaps. An outbreak of stomach sickness. A man overboard. Don't you agree?'

'Up to a point,' said Tudor. 'But on the whole people come on the *Duchess* to get away from that sort of unpleasantness. It's like country-house weekends. People didn't go away expecting to find a body in the library, a suspicious butler, an adulterous hostess and Miss Marple or Monsieur Poirot asking a lot of impertinent questions and coming up with some embarrassing answers. They just wanted to play billiards and croquet, drink champagne and flirt. Same with being on board the *Duchess*. Passengers come for a quiet life — eat, drink, be quietly merry, tango with a gentleman host or a beautiful passenger and generally escape unpleasant reality.'

'My turn to say 'up to a point',' said Doctor Umlaut, smiling, 'and to observe that life isn't like that. A truism verging on a cliché. There is a sense that a great ship is a microcosm of the greater life in the world outside. Not unlike the country-house you describe. And if reality should rear its ugly head it is much more difficult to escape its clutches on board ship than on dry land. Perhaps that is a paradox too.'

He's trying to tell me something, thought Tudor, but he's being so elliptical that I'm not sure what he means. He wasn't altogether sure that Umlaut himself knew.

'What I mean to say,' said the little man, seeming to sense the lack of comprehension and the ambiguity that had caused it, 'is that nothing is ever what it seems and never more so than in an isolated, hot-house atmosphere such as this, from which, for a while at least, there is no escape. But you will know this from your academic studies. Forgive me. I am presuming too much, encroaching on an area of expertise which is foreign to me just as it is familiar to you.'

Tudor nodded his head but said nothing.

'And,' Doctor Umlaut abruptly changed

the subject, 'talking of academic interests. I thought your talk on HMS *Bounty* most interesting. What is your next subject please?'

'Piracy,' said Tudor. 'Tomorrow at eleven.'

Doctor Umlaut inclined his head. 'I have often wondered,' he said, 'about the exact distinction between privateers, buccaneers and pirates.'

'It can be a perilously thin line,' said Tudor, 'but in essence an act of piracy is when a ship is seized out of control of her legal master and crew by those who have boarded the vessel in disguise as passengers. When captured they were hanged in chains on prominent headlands as a warning to others. Or staked to the ground at Execution Dock in Wapping to be drowned by the rising tide.'

Mrs Umlaut let out a little yelp of disgust but her husband seemed quite amused.

'The last pirate was executed in England in 1840,' added Tudor, 'but the United States executed one in 1862.'

Doctor Umlaut shook his charred head and smiled.

Tudor half-expected him to say '*Ach so!*' which was almost exactly what he did, adding the single line, 'History is so often an act of repetition, don't you think? Even at sea there is nothing new under the sun.'

22

Angus Donaldson's cabin shook, trembled and rattled causing Tudor to quite involuntarily do much the same.

'We seem to be making good speed,' said Tudor.

'Aye,' said Donaldson, who was a man of few words save when cracking ancient jokes over the Tannoy. He hailed from the Kingdom of Fife and was loose-limbed and bearded. His family were all fisher-folk and his brother and nephews still manned a small herring trawler in the town of Anstruther. Angus had come south and been with Riviera Shipping most of his adult life.

'Should be in New York on schedule if not before,' said Tudor conversationally.

'Happen,' said Donaldson.

They were both standing and Donaldson suddenly and awkwardly motioned his guest to sit. They both did so. The Staff Captain's cabin had two armchairs, upright and not particularly comfortable. Donaldson did not offer his guest any refreshment. Instead he said, 'I'd like to extend the company's thanks in the matter of apprehending the ruffians who attempted to hijack the vessel.'

He was not only a man of few words, he had a funny way with them.

There was a black and white masked ball in the Great Hall that evening and Tudor was already wearing his black tie and dinner jacket which seemed a marginal cop-out but could hardly be more black and white. His bog-standard black mask, purchased in the ship's boutique was in his pocket. For the time being he was instantly recognizable.

'That's very kind of you,' said Tudor. 'Thank you.'

The Staff Captain flashed an official smile of acknowledgement and then said, a touch ominously, 'But.'

The monosyllable hung in the air between them for what seemed like a long time. Then Donaldson repeated it making it seem even worse second time round.

'That will be all. It was Ms Goldslinger's initiative to embroil you in the unpleasantness that occurred earlier and I'm afraid she exceeded her authority. No harm done fortunately, but from now on the proprieties will be observed and Riviera Shipping will take care of things in the normal way.'

'You can't behave 'in the normal way',' protested Tudor, 'when events just aren't normal.'

The Staff Captain shrugged. 'Riviera Shipping is prepared for every eventuality,' he said, as if reciting from an instruction manual.

Tudor shrugged back but could think of no immediately sensible riposte. It was abundantly clear that the company was not prepared for every eventuality. The Irish had taken it by surprise: Tudor had saved its bacon. Now the captain was off sick believed missing, and the ring-leader of the pirates had escaped. A key passenger had almost been incinerated. An empty lifeboat had been recovered with hundreds of thousands of pounds-worth of gold ingots and possibly a blood-stain. Ashley Carpenter had planted an obituary notice of his good self. There was nothing normal in any of this and, as far as he could see, the official response had been non-existent. No wonder Donaldson shrugged. A collective shrug seemed to be the official reaction. Not good enough in his estimation.

'Anyway,' said Donaldson, 'while thanking you for your valuable assistance I must point out, again on behalf of the company, that you are engaged solely as a guest speaker so that while we appreciate your continued efforts in that capacity we must ask that you in no way exceed or deviate from the terms of your contract.'

'Say again,' said Tudor, in the vernacular he had picked up from the crew's communication. No one in the navy seemed ever to use the word 'repeat'.

'I say again,' said Donaldson, 'stick to what you've been hired to do. Lecture the passengers. Understood?'

He made it sound very like a threat and Tudor finally took the hint, made only the flimsiest pretext of an excuse, and left.

★ ★ ★

The masked or was it 'masqued' ball that followed was as surreal an affair as he had expected and feared. He and Elizabeth had bought the most basic Venetian-style masks from Ye Shoppe situated aft on the boat deck. Ye Shoppe had obviously bought a job lot of such things from a manufacturer with an obscurely Middle Eastern sounding name in Skegness. The masks were heavily scquinned and came in two kinds. One was a sort of permanent business of the type airlines provided to shut out light when attempting to sleep and came with elastic bands which fitted over the ears. These not only left your hands free for dancing, or whatever, and would have been useful for gentleman hosts attempting to prevent their leaning partners from toppling over. They also ensured that the disguise did not slip. The other kind came on sticks like sartorial lollipops. They were cheaper, meant that at least one hand had to be kept clutching it and were imperfect at hiding one's identity. In other words these masks slipped.

Music was provided by the ship's resident band, the Dukes of Dixie, an elderly gaggle of jazz musicians who had originally played together in the far-off days of Radio Luxemburg. Transferring to the later pirate radio ship, *Caroline*, moored for a while in the middle of the North Sea the Dukes had rather taken to the ocean wave so that when she was launched the *Duchess* was, in every way, made for them. Once svelte, lean and darkly handsome, the Dukes had become grey, tubby and mildly seedy, but they could still hold a tune and belt it out satisfactorily. Their lead singer who called himself Hiram G. Billy, but whose real name was something quite different, could have rasped a bronchial rap with George Melly who must have been much the same age.

The dancers seemed, on the whole, to have some difficulty keeping up with the Dukes but that didn't really matter much. Meanwhile, waiters shimmered about the ballroom with sparkling drinks of uncertain provenance and the ship rolled.

'If Mom and Dad could see me now,' muttered Elizabeth, as she led Tudor round the floor and peeked over the top of her hand-held mask.

'I know what you mean,' said her partner, perspiring. It seemed awfully hot to him though not, apparently, to everyone else.

From time to time passing dancers waved, bowed or in other ways made themselves known to Tudor and Elizabeth. This was polite but tantalizing since without exception they appeared to have masks which worked and which in many cases seemed to have come from more exotic and expensive places than Ye Shoppe or Skegness.

Much of this dress was decidedly fancy so that Tudor in his regulation dinner jacket and Elizabeth in her almost equally regulation little black dress felt ill-prepared and out-of-place. They were not real cruisers in the sense that the majority of the *Duchess*'s passengers clearly were. They lacked the wardrobe and they grew restless with too much indolence and pleasure. Most of the disguised dancers, however, were having a ball.

'Who *are* all these people?' asked Elizabeth, as they shuffled round the small and undulating floor. 'I mean have we, like, been introduced?'

The Dukes seemed to accelerate their syncopations as if to emphasize their difference from the paying passengers. Quick, quick, slow seemed to become fast, fast, quick but it made little apparent difference to the gentlemen hosts, their partners and those who followed. They stuck to their own time and beat which was, of course, a great deal more leisurely than the Dukes' geriatric frenzy. Sticking to their own time and beat was, Tudor reflected, what passengers did best. The *Duchess* had guidelines which needed to be adhered to but within these confines her clientele did pretty much as they pleased in their own distinctive fashions. It was, up to a point, the purpose of cruising.

From time to time fellow-revellers bumped into Tudor and Elizabeth or they into them. Because, however, they were masked neither Tudor nor his partners knew who they were. This, Tudor supposed, was another of cruising's golden rules. One was always bumping into people. You were seldom sure who they were and the odds were that you would never see them again. This didn't matter for they were ships that pass in the night. Or to be precise, they were *on* ships that pass in the night. Or to be even more precise, they were *like* ships that pass in the night.

'Ouch!' exclaimed Elizabeth. 'You just trod on my toe.'

'Sorry,' he said. 'I wasn't thinking.'

'Yes, you were,' she riposted. 'Thinking too much. You may not be the niftiest dancer ever known but you're not a foot-treader. Penny for them.'

'What?'

'The thoughts.'

The band was playing something Tudor thought dimly was by Gershwin though one Dukes' melody sounded pretty much like another. They were that sort of band and made that sort of noise. Syncopated muzak. Rentabilk.

'I don't know,' he said, 'I was all over the place.'

'Including my feet,' said Elizabeth with feeling, though less feeling than a few moments earlier when Tudor had first stepped on them.

One of Prince Abdullah's wives cannoned off them and bounced away at around forty-five degrees giggling coquettishly. She was, surprisingly, locked in a stiff embrace with an obvious gentleman host in a vaguely Mexican-eagle head-dress and mask. The Aztec eagle had the hallmarks — tottering dexterity, louche innocence — of Ambrose Perry but then so many of the gentlemen

237

hosts were similar walking oxymorons. The girl might not have been one of Abdullah's brides but she wore a jellaba — which obviated the need for a mask — and Tudor was so influenced by the clichés of shipboard life that he had begun jumping to conclusions he would never have reached on shore. Whatever, the girl had dancing eyes and seemed familiar. Tudor had an odd sense that the Prince's harem was increasing every knot. It was as if they were multiplying by some strange osmotic reproductive process. This could have been an illusion.

The band seemed to be playing 'The Eton Boating Song' souped up. Presumably a Humphrey Lyttleton adaptation created perhaps for a Beaulieu jazz festival of the 1950s. It was like all the other noises made by the band but somewhere in among the farty-brassy stridences you could just about make out the plangent notes of the old rowing number with its references to jollity and togetherness which seemed apt and to 'feathering' which didn't.

Mandy Goldslinger slunk past, facially disguised but instantly recognizable on account of her constricted and cantilevered carcass entubed in sequins and lamé and doing something mildly South American with a black-masked figure in the uniform of a ship's doctor. She waved a touch too gaily. The game Doctor and Frau Umlaut, recognizable by their singes, limped past forlornly. Prince Abdullah sat on a sofa surveying the hordes, smoking implacably.

'Mass murderers,' said Tudor. 'Looking around here I'd say they might all have done it.'

'That's silly,' said Elizabeth.

'Maybe,' said Tudor. 'But it's life and death as well. Nearly everyone prancing around this room is capable of murder.'

'So what?' Elizabeth had to shout in to his ear as they shuffled round the Great Hall, 'We're all *capable* of murder. Ashley taught me that and you say the same. But as you also say, the fact that we're *capable* of murder doesn't make us all murderers. We could all commit all sorts of crimes but that doesn't turn us into criminals. Civilization is about the suppression of instinct. If we all did what we could and, more importantly, if we all did what we'd really like then life would be impossible. We'd all be killing each other, nicking each other's possessions, having sex with each other's partners and Christ knows what.'

The band had moved on to 'Amazing Grace'. Strange how they managed to make the same noise all the time and yet underlay it with a just recognizable tune.

'I still think the room is full of potential killers,' said Tudor, as they cannoned off a couple who had the ample paunch and posterior of the Goronwy Watkyns. Whoever they were they made no acknowledgement of acquaintance but waddled off, wiggling, more or less in time to the music.

'That's silly too,' said Elizabeth. 'I think you've overdone it. I think you should go to bed.'

'I do feel tired,' said Tudor. 'It's been a rough old day. But I still think there's more murder and more crime at sea than most people admit. Which means that there are plenty of criminals afloat. And plenty right here all round us, thinly disguised or not.'

'Bed,' she said, 'definitely time for bed.'

And for a fleeting moment Tudor thought he caught a whiff of double-entendre.

23

Once more he slept fitfully. This actually meant that he tossed and turned and had trouble breathing when on his back and even more when he turned over and tried lying on his stomach. The ship was noisy and the ride bumpy but neither of these was the problem. He slept well on ships, even in storms and this wasn't a storm in the accepted sense. He was dog-tired as well so sleep should have come easily, but somehow it didn't. Once or twice he got up and peered out of the port hole, awed as usual, by the vast expanse of white capped nothingness of the mid-Atlantic.

Donaldson's words bothered him. In a sense they were not new. He had been living with the strictures of hard-bitten professionals for the whole of his working life. Back home, his old mucker Trythall was permanently on his shoulder, a copper's copper now holding the exalted rank of Detective Chief Inspector in the local constabulary. Trythall had always taken an avuncular view: OK sonny, abstract theories are all very well in your ivory tower, but when it comes to real life you should leave it to real men like me — people who've actually been out on the beat, felt a few collars, witnessed nature red in tooth and claw, been there and done that. You stick to your books and papers, your lectures and tutorials. You're fiction: we're fact.

He sighed up at the ceiling. Dawn was breaking through the night outside and forcing lightness through the porthole. Newer ships had square windows and balconies. The *Duchess* belonged to a different generation when seaworthiness was the first consideration in ship-building. She was almost defiantly old-fashioned and seaworthy. A professional to her fingertips.

Which brought him back to his sleep-disturbing unease. Was he a genuine professional? Of course he was. He ran a fine department in an adequate university. It was, in fact, a flagship outfit — an alpha institution in an otherwise beta organization. He personally enjoyed international respect among his peers. He had a job and he was good at it. His alumni prospered. Likewise his papers and pamphlets. He teetered on the brink of celebrity, was already world-famous in Wessex. And yet, deep down in his heart of hearts, he feared that men like Trythall and Donaldson were right. He was an amateur and they were professionals; he was a Gentleman and they were Players.

He got up again and went to the porthole. Away in the distance he could make out a huge container ship buffeting through the waves. He was reminded of John Masefield's catchy little poem 'Cargoes' which he had learned by heart as a child. They hadn't had container ships in Masefield's day, just chunky little tramp steamers with cargoes of pig-iron. That wasn't quite right. Pig-lead. He closed his eyes.

Funny, he could have sworn it was 'pig-iron' not 'pig-lead' and a 'Tramp steamer' not a 'coaster.' Just showed how fallible memory was and yet memory was a cornerstone of conventional British justice. Evidence in court was memory-based, almost by definition. Yet memory was almost always flawed. Tramp steamers, he thought, squinting at the ugly container vessel on the horizon, had been consigned to history along with bobbies on bicycles. Somehow everything seemed to bring him back to police procedure. He supposed he must have learned the Masefield at about the time that he was first getting to know Sherlock Holmes and Lord Peter Wimsey. Privately he still stuck to the belief that these two were the best detectives ever with Holmes right out in front of Wimsey, and the rest limping along in their wake. As for real-life detectives they were nothing compared to the giants of fiction. Whisper it not to the likes of Donaldson and Trythall but they were mere pygmies in the police pantheon.

Day really was beginning to dawn now. He realized as he watched fingers of pink illuminating the ocean that it had been a while since they had seen the sun or even a hint of blue sky. They had been sailing under and over steel grey. A metaphor for life, he thought gloomily. His existence was seldom punctuated even by shafts of crepuscular pink but was almost uniformly monotone. No, that was an exaggeration. There were a number of highs in his life of lows but in the still small hours it never seemed like that, particularly after a dressing down from a man such as Angus Donaldson. He knew he should rise above such sermons but he was absurdly thin-skinned besides which there was more than a shadow of doubt about the worth of what he was doing. In his heart of hearts he doubted even whether Wessex should have a university of its own and whether, anyway, the University of Wessex was worthy of the name. His department was degree-giving. You could graduate with a Bachelor of Arts in Criminal Studies or even, God help him, a Ph.D. in Criminal Studies complete with tasselled mortar board and a banana and orange hood to your rook-like black gown. Was it all a farce? The Vice-Chancellor had even tried to foist Lord Archer of Weston-super-Mare on him as one of a batch of celebrity honorary ordinands but at least Tudor had been able to resist that one. No honorary degree from Wessex for Jeffrey. Not even over his dead body.

He sat down heavily on the bed. Now there was a success. Lord Archer of Weston-super-Mare. He was a real pro. But here Tudor really did tell himself to take a grip. There were crimes to consider, disappearances to be explained and he really could not afford the luxury of contemplating Jeffrey Archer.

He supposed he should do as he was commanded by Donaldson. After all the man was in charge of the ship and had a right to be obeyed without question. That was the way they did things in the Merchant Marine. You did as you were told without demur. If there was to be a debate you had to wait until after the event. Quite unlike civvy street and in particular to a man such as Tudor Cornwall whose natural instinct honed by years of practice was to subject everything to relentless, forensic examination.

Someone knocked on the door and he glanced at his watch. 6.30. Far too early for room service even if he had ordered such a thing. He presumed it was a human knock and not a ship's rodent scratching. If it were human it could be an enemy, dangerous. *Tipperary Tatler* perhaps still dangerously at large. Or someone suspicious like Freddie Grim or Prince Abdullah or . . . well, as he had observed on the dance floor of the Great Hall the previous night, almost everyone was more or less suspicious. He simply couldn't afford to be paranoid and terrified of every early morning knock on the door. Nevertheless caution was advisable.

'Who is it?' he asked in a stage whisper.

'It's me,' said a strong, female Antipodean voice, 'Elizabeth.'

'Oh,' he replied, apprehensive though not for quite the same fearful reasons as a few seconds earlier. 'What is it?'

'I wanted to see you. Let me in. The door's locked.'

He put on a *Duchess* towelling bath robe with the ship's logo of anchor and tiara over the breast pocket, unlocked the door and admitted a windblown waif in tight jeans and a turquoise tank top. She was blue lips, tousled hair and damp, salty spray.

'Brill sunrise,' she said. 'I've been up on the foredeck or whatever you call it. You know, just under the bridge. I was the only person there. It was just miraculous. One minute it's so dark you can still see the stars and that container ship away on the left was still lit up — '

'Port,' said Tudor pedantically.

'You what?'

'Port,' he said. 'On board ship left is port and right is starboard.'

'That's just affectation,' she said. 'Any case you no more know your port from your starboard than your arse from your elbow. You're even more of a landlubber than I am.'

'It's not an affectation actually,' said Tudor, uncomfortably aware that he was sounding even more pompous. 'If you say 'right' or 'left' there's room for ambiguity. If you're facing the stern it could be your left or the ship's left. If it's port or starboard it's always the same. See what I mean? Did you say you were watching the sunrise over the bows. You sure you don't mean the stern?'

'Unlike you,' she said, 'I do know my arse from my elbow, my port from my starboard and, above all and most certainly, my bows from my stern and my front from your back.'

'And you saw the sun come up while you were standing forrard.'

'Amazing. First of all you just have a sort of general pink haze and then this amazing sort of red cricket ball emerges and pops up. It's like a beachball being squeezed out of a swimming pool. You know? Now you see it, now you don't. Or rather, the other way around. Now you don't see it, then you do. Exciting. It almost fizzed. First real sun I've seen all trip.'

'You sure you were in the bows?'

'Don't be silly. Look on the TV.'

The TV set had no fewer than eighteen channels. Half a dozen were dedicated to movies; three to a loop of in-house lecturing, including Tudor himself — to his chagrin; others were devoted to sales of various *Duchess*-related products including shore excursions where appropriate. Channel Three was 'The View from the Bridge' with classical music. Tudor turned it on and was rewarded by Handel and a magnificent view of the sharp end of the *Duchess* ploughing towards a gloriously rising sun. 'Thine be the Glory' Judas Maccabeus. Epic stuff.

'See,' said Elizabeth. 'Stern indeed. Did we have a bet on it?'

'Not that I can remember. You can have a second boiled egg for breakfast.'

'Big bloody deal,' she grinned. 'I slept like a log till six. How about you?'

''Fraid not,' he said. 'Donaldson's slightly got to me. I have a feeling we should pull back; leave things to sort themselves out; let

Donaldson and his security team take care of it all.'

'Security team!?' Elizabeth looked sexily angry. 'Those goons! You must be joking.'

'To be honest I hadn't given them much thought. But my strong impression is that Donaldson is concerned to try to keep a lid on the situation; prevent things getting out of hand; hand it over to competent authorities as soon as possible.'

'And you feel like letting him?'

Tudor shrugged. 'If I'm asked to help — as I was by Mandy Goldslinger — then I'll do what I can. But if I'm expressly told not to interfere I don't feel I have much alternative.'

'That's a bit weedy.'

'It's life,' he said. 'When the chips are down I have to admit that I have no authority. Also my skills are essentially theoretical. You could be the regius professor of law at Oxford or whatever but that doesn't mean that you'd be competent to lead for the prosecution or defence at a big case at the Old Bailey.'

'On the contrary,' said Elizabeth, 'you'd be a damned sight better than most barristers. You always say so and I believe you. I think you're right. I also think you'd make a better first of conducting a criminal investigation. Probably better than the average senior cop back in the UK and most certainly than some jumped up security guard on board ship.'

'I don't know,' he said, 'we're all prone to self-doubt. I'm all very well on paper, lecturing, sitting in my ivory tower. But sometimes I feel I should stay there and leave real life to the people who deal with real life. I just do theory and I should stick to it.'

'Well, maybe,' she said, 'but I think you have a duty to be involved. 'We have every reason to believe that Sam Hardy, the legitimately appointed Master of the *Duchess* has been removed from his position against his will and possibly even murdered. I think you have a perfect right — duty even — to insist on his being released or produced. And until and unless that's done you should investigate like fury.'

'It's not as simple as that,' he said, glancing at his watch. 'They'll be serving breakfast in a moment and I'm feeling peckish. I'm going to have a shave and a shower then I'll see you up there. If you're there ahead of me I'll have porridge and a couple of boiled eggs with brown toast and black coffee.'

'And mine's mixed berries, low fat yoghurt and camomile tea,' she said, letting herself out. 'I guess you could poison us with any of that, though my money's on the dispenser which 'sanitizes' your hands. That's a murder weapon if ever I saw one. Sir Goronwy Watkyn in the Chatsworth with the hand-sanitizer. Beats Colonel Mustard in the conservatory with the lead piping any day.'

And she laughed.

24

Breakfast aboard the *Duchess* was always a muted, even subdued, affair. The morning after the masked ball it was, inevitably, even quieter and more sparsely populated than usual.

The meal was served between 7 and 9.30 but that was ship's time which by now was in a little warp all of its own. In the middle — or thereabouts — of its voyage to the United States, the *Duchess* was chronologically behind home but ahead of her destination. She lost an hour a day throughout the voyage, so that by the time she arrived in New York, she was five miles behind her base in the United Kingdom and existing at the same time as the millions of Americans living along the Eastern Seaboard. In mid-Atlantic she was as isolated in time terms as she was geographically. This compounded her sense of loneliness, isolation and vulnerability. In terms of the ideal setting for a closed-room classic Agatha Christie murder she knocked a snow-bound country house into any number of cocked hats.

In a real terrestrial stately home, of course,

there would have been a hotplate on a sideboard with silver topped dishes of kidneys and kedgeree from which silent guests would have helped themselves. The *Duchess* was more grand hotel than grande dame with what the trade called 'silver service' from waiters and waitresses with names such as Waclav and Natalia, all immaculate in starched jackets and with manners and skills that their United Kingdom counterparts simply couldn't have deployed. Tudor found this mildly depressing though not sufficiently to put him off his boiled eggs which came just as he preferred with firm whites, gungy yolks and crisp brown soldiers. Elizabeth dabbed at a light moustache of low-fat yoghurt and eyed him disapprovingly.

The crew to passenger ratio on board the ship was amazingly high. There were almost as many people driving the ship and attending to the clients' needs as there were paying punters. Given that the passengers were for the most part elderly and infirm and the crew fit and youthful it would have been a doddle for a mutiny to have succeeded. Overpowering resistance, should the masses behind the green baize door have risen up in rebellion, would have been ridiculously easy. Over the years Tudor had witnessed some ugly moments when passengers took against crew or, less obviously, vice versa. But none had ended in tears.

'That's a heart attack on a plate,' said Elizabeth virtuously.

'Nonsense,' said Tudor. 'Two *not* hard boiled eggs represent a mild palpitation at worst. Fay Weldon as much as said so. 'Go to work on an egg'.'

'That was an advertising campaign on behalf of the Egg Marketing Board if I'm correctly informed,' she said. 'But for a man of your age and in your condition they're a bad idea in anything other than moderation.'

'I can't help my age,' said Tudor, 'but there is nothing at all wrong with my condition. I'm in perfectly good nick. And certainly in good enough nick not to be damaged by a couple of boiled eggs for breakfast.'

She seemed unimpressed.

'Boiled eggs are bad for you,' she said. 'End of story. But more to the point, 'Are you a detective or not?' People like Trythall and Donaldson are right in a way. You're all fur coat and no knickers. Most of the time, operating in the UK the way you do you're in the same position as a critic to an author or a concert. Power possibly, but no responsibility. Now here, for once, you're outside police jurisdiction, away from the rule of law, you have a serious possibility of showing the world that you're not just a load of hot air but a real power to be reckoned with. This is a serious chance to prove yourself. Take it, run with it, come first past the post and you're made for life — fail and everyone's criticism is justified.'

'That's pretty harsh.'

'It's life,' she said, smiling.

'A defining moment?'

'You could say that.'

'If I cop out I remain a peripheral figure, properly despised by those at the sharp end like Detective Chief Superintendent Trythall and Captain Donaldson.'

'You said it.' She spooned low-fat yoghurt on to her berries, blue, black, straw, rasp. Waclav poured her more camomile tea. Natalia poured him more black coffee.

Away in the distance the Umlauts, still charred, were breakfasting off cured herring, pumpernickel and Darjeeling tea with lemon. They seemed agitated and presently Walter placed his napkin carefully to the left of his place, pushed back his chair and walked slowly to Tudor and Elizabeth's table where he asked if he might sit. They naturally acquiesced.

'You understand, naturally,' he began, 'that the man Abdullah and I are not the best of friends.'

No one said anything.

'Enemies, in fact.'

Tudor and Elizabeth both nodded.

'He is not, of course, a prince.'

There seemed nothing they could say and they didn't, though Elizabeth smiled encouragingly.

'And his wives are not wives.'

'Really!' said Tudor. 'I've had my suspicions about the so-called wives ever since we set sail.'

Elizabeth shot him a glance which was half amused, half exasperated. It seemed to say 'Men!'

'And they have been multiplying,' said Dr Umlaut. Waclav asked if he'd like something to drink and he said he'd like to continue with Darjeeling and a slice of lemon.

'Multiplying?' asked Tudor.

'There are now more than there were when we embarked,' he said. 'I can't say for certain how many more but there has been a definite increase. You know that Abdullah is attempting to acquire the ship and make it his own. With compulsory smoking everywhere.'

'I understood as much,' said Tudor, 'but I understand that you too aspire to taking over the ship.'

'Only in order to prevent this horrible person,' said the Doctor. 'My position is entirely, as you would have it, reactive. If this so-called 'Prince' were not in the frame I would be more than content to let the status quo maintain itself.'

'Well that's by the by,' said Tudor. 'The fact is that you and Prince Abdullah, Prince or not, are in the middle of what is, in effect a boardroom war. From a seat in the grandstand it's quite difficult to call the shots. As an impartial observer I . . . well let's just say I find it very difficult to become partial. I'm not sure I should take sides.'

'But there is good,' said Umlaut, 'which is me. And there is bad, which is that man.'

'With respect,' said Tudor, meaning as always when those words are uttered, nothing of the sort, 'we only have your word for that.'

'My word is my bond,' said the little man, bristling in a burnt-out way.

'That too. This wouldn't stand up in court. You need proof, corroborative evidence.'

'That's what we look to you for. You are our resident expert. You run a department of criminal affairs at a university. You are the expert. Much better than police. They have no brain.'

'It's very kind of you to say so,' said Tudor, 'but I'm afraid I'm off the case. The captain has ordered me to back off.'

'But we have no captain. The captain is

missing. This is the heart of the mystery. This is why you are essential. It is you who must discover the body. Or the living person. We rely on you. The whole ship relies on you.' He sounded quite distraught.

'The drill is that the senior officer aboard is the man in charge. The official line is that the Master himself is indisposed due to laryngitis. Because he can't speak the captaincy automatically devolves on to his number two, Angus Donaldson. That means that Donaldson is in charge. And Donaldson has ordered me off the case. Whatever you or I think about that it really leaves me with no options. Sorry.'

Waclav brought a pot of Darjeeling and some lemon slices. The three of them sat in silence while he poured.

When he had retreated, Umlaut said, 'I also am sorry.'

'I'm not sure I agree with your sit rep,' said Elizabeth. 'If you have good reason to believe that the right and proper captain of the ship, namely Sam Hardy, has been abducted, maybe even murdered, and that Angus Donaldson might conceivably have been involved in the crime, then surely you're duty bound to solve the mystery no matter what. If Donaldson's position as *de facto*, substitute boss has been wrongfully obtained then all bets are off. I'm not convinced Donaldson has the right to tell you what to do.'

'Mind if I join you?' It was Mandy Goldslinger looking as if she had slept as fitfully as Tudor. She had rings under her eyes, her hands shook and her voice sounded husky.

'Tomato juice, Waclav,' she said, 'heavy on the Tabasco and Worcester. Very black coffee.' She sat down without waiting for a say-so.

'Couldn't help hearing that,' she said, 'and I agree and then again I don't. If it's any consolation I've had a shot across the bows from Donaldson just like Tudor has. And according to the rules he has authority on his side. I mean he's the number two and there's no number one and therefore in the absence of the said number one the number two takes the top spot. Do I make myself clear?'

'Not entirely,' said Tudor, 'but I think we call get your drift.'

'On the other hand,' continued the Cruise Director, 'if the number two has only got into pole position on account of nefarious behaviour towards his superior officer and captain then all bets are off and it's permissible to investigate. Not just permissible but imperative.'

'May an old man pull up a chair?'

It was Sir Goronwy Watkyn looking as if he

had enjoyed a better night's sleep than anyone.

' 'It appears,' he said, extracting an empty chair from an adjacent table, 'that willy-nilly we find ourselves as players in the sort of puzzle in which I and the good Doctor here' — he nodded almost conspiratorially in the direction of Tudor Cornwall — 'specialize — though usually as arbiters rather than participants.'

'We are together here whether we like it or not,' said Umlaut. 'It is inescapable. We are in on the act. We are on stage. We cannot just be in the audience.'

'Our friend has a certain logic on his side,' said Sir Goronwy portentous as ever. 'In life on land an inspector calls. In a situation such as this, one dials nine nine nine and policemen arrive, lawyers are retained and the whole apparatus of detection, apprehension, trial and sentence is gone through in the traditional manner. Out here however we are in, as it were, a nautical jungle. There are no policemen, no lawyers, no trials, no juries. On this occasion, quite fortuitously, we have a number of experts of whom I have the honour to be one. This expertise should be utilized. We would be failing in our duty if we were to do otherwise and particularly if we were to stand idly by.'

'But,' protested Tudor, 'we have absolutely no legal authority. Besides, in a day or so the ship will be docking and the whole matter can be handed over to the legitimate authorities.'

'But those authorities will be American,' said Umlaut, 'and the ship is registered in the United Kingdom. This presents the first of many dilemmas. The pirates are, I believe, Irish. American justice is, as you say, notoriously one-eyed with regard to the Emerald Isle. The Abdullah man comes from I know not where. So where does this leave us? In a state of much confusion. I certainly am in such a state.'

'Seems to me,' said Elizabeth, 'that Donaldson is, on the one hand a prime suspect, and on the other, judge and jury. That's not right.'

They all thought about this while the staff replenished their drinks.

'I don't trust Donaldson,' said Mandy Goldslinger, 'and I fear for Sam.' She seemed tearful.

Tudor pushed his chair back. 'I'm sorry,' he said. 'I'm sure you'll forgive me but I have a lecture to deliver at eleven and I need to prepare. Also I have a letter to write.'

He smiled around at the little group which seemed dissatisfied if not exactly open-mouthed. He glanced out of the window — a big square job at this more exalted level than his stateroom. Outside the day had turned sullen gun-metal grey and the sky was quite without features.

25

His talk on pirates seemed to go reasonably well. He had done it many times before and was able to speak for forty-five minutes or so without notes. The producer in the box at the back of the theatre was an old acquaintance now and trusted him not to do anything ridiculous, to keep his voice level consistent, speak slowly, and perhaps above all not to attempt anything too ambitious on the joke front. There were between 100 and 150 in the audience which was marginally more than for his 'Mutiny on the *Bounty*' lecture. He decided on a blazer with an open-necked shirt which seemed to him to combine informality and gravitas to more or less the right degree. He used a hand-held mike and walked about on the stage, pausing occasionally to sit but not, as some speakers, did, venturing down into the actual auditorium. That, he considered, was too Billy Graham.

One or two of his listeners went to sleep or at least closed their eyes and opened their mouths which might, or might not, have been the same. He spotted Freddie Grim and his wife; Ambrose Perry and at least one

Abdullah 'wife' though not the Prince himself. No Umlaut, no Goldslinger, no Watkyns and no Elizabeth. They could have been continuing their post-breakfast discussions or merely skipped his talk. Elizabeth, at least, had heard it several times before.

Mid-morning was prime time for speaking because on the whole the passengers had not yet had recourse to the bottle. Any time after lunch was bad, though evenings were worst. Mercifully this was not a lecture time zone and the après-dinner slots were all filled by stand-up comics and dancers who reported whole rows of passengers sleeping off the evening meal in preparation for the midnight buffet. In the middle of the morning audiences were inclined to be, relatively speaking, wide awake.

When he finished there was a ripple of polite applause and he took two or three questions. He always dreaded questions on the grounds that they would either be wince-makers such as 'Do you write under your own name?' or even, most shaming of all 'What did you say your name was?' or, arguably worse, would come from someone who knew more about pirates than he did or even, God save him, was a pirate or retired pirate him or herself. 'Thus when I boarded a cargo ship called *Polaris* in the Malacca

Strait ... ' or 'Out of two hundred and thirty-seven reported incidents of piracy in the Indian Ocean last year how many would you say ... '

Mercifully on this occasion the questions were all placid half-volleys along the lines of 'Why Blue Beard and not some other colour?' and 'Is there a future for piracy?' These were easily swatted away and when he had finished he received another round of applause warmer than the first.

As the audience filed out for early cocktails one of them headed for the stage and as he came down the steps into the body of the hall came up very close and whispered in a breathy almost stage-Irish, 'Great talk, Dr Cornwall. Now just smile at me bravely and make a show of saying something sensible. But don't try anything silly or you're dead meat.'

It was an Abdullah wife, but masquerading under the anonymity-conferring robes was none other than the missing girl herself, *Tipperary Tatler*.

She prodded him in the ribs with something metallic feeling. 'This is loaded,' she said, 'and I shan't hesitate to use it.'

'You wouldn't dare,' he said.

They were alone in the theatre now. The lights were dim. The sound box and projectionist's room were empty too. It was just the two of them. If she were to carry out her threat and shoot him dead she would have no difficulty in getting away and vanishing back into the safety of the Prince's harem. The threat was real. Tudor thought of calling the bluff but decided that it would be the silly side of valour. He had no wish to end his life shot dead in the theatre of the *Duchess* after one of his talks. People would say it was a more than usually disappointed member of his audience expressing disgust. That would taint the obituaries. Seriously, he told himself, there was no point in taking unnecessary risks. Besides he had sent his letter which was the nearest he could think of to an SOS for Eddie Trythall. He wondered if it would get through.

'Try me,' said the woman. 'I'm perfectly happy to pull the trigger and I'm quite confident I'd get clean away. If not then *tant pis*. The Americans will be thoroughly understanding. Unlike the Brits. They like us. Now just walk normally and naturally out the door and turn left. I'll keep guiding you.'

Tudor shrugged and did as he was told. On balance he didn't think he had a serious alternative. Outside the library they almost bumped into Freddie Grim who smiled and gave him an odd look but said nothing.

Tipperary obviously sensed trouble for she gave him a snarling jab with the gun — always supposing it was a gun. It could have been anything, but Tudor still reckoned it was not a bluff worth calling. Besides he was curious. Once the ship lurched unexpectedly and Tudor stumbled. The woman jabbed him again and hissed an obscenity. They took the stairs upwards and then walked forward along the boat deck before cutting inside.

Finally they reached what was clearly their destination. The door said 'Captain. Private'. Tudor arched an eyebrow as the woman took a key from her pocket, opened the door, gave Tudor a shove in the back which propelled him inside, closed the door behind him and disappeared. Tudor was not at all sure what or whom to expect but it was lax of him not to expect the disarmingly but unconvincingly friendly figure he found in front of him sitting at the captain's desk scribbling something on a notepad.

'Tudor,' said the man, tall, lean, fifty something, in corduroy trousers and a tweed jacket with a roll-neck sweater. He looked what he was: a provincial academic. But what he really was, was Tudor's nemesis; his Moriarty, the blast from the past who was not at all what he had seemed and had come back to haunt him on what now seemed to be a regular basis.

'Ashley,' he said, trying to appear unfazed as if encountering his former undergraduate contemporary and friend was the most natural thing in all the world. Maybe it was. Ashley had become the bad penny in his life. He was always turning up when least expected and least wanted. Why not now?

The basic facts about Ashley were simple enough. He and Tudor had been contemporaries at Oxford University many years ago and had both entered academic life as young dons in criminal affairs departments on opposite sides of the world: Ashley in Australia whence he came; Tudor in the UK. From time to time their paths had crossed, mainly at academic conferences in different parts of the globe but inevitably they drifted apart. Then, suddenly, out of the blue, Ashley had invited Tudor to be Visiting Fellow in his faculty at university in Tasmania. Tudor accepted but when he arrived Ashley had vanished without explanation. He reappeared but not before a woman had been murdered by a form of remote control and Tudor was suspected of the crime. Only then did Ashley return, determined, apparently, to have his old 'friend' convicted. He failed. Tudor returned to the University of Wessex but found that he had acquired a formidably bright Ph.D. student in Elizabeth Burney, former protégée and erstwhile mistress of Ashley himself. Elizabeth seemed to have changed sides and had been loyal and clever ever since the transition. But there was always the possibility, embedded deep and immovably in Tudor's sub-conscious — that she was some form of sleeper. One day perhaps she would be 'activated' by Ashley and used against him.

Quite what had motivated this late flowering lust for revenge was quite beyond Tudor. It was too simple and unrigorous to simply shrug and say that he must have gone mad. But there was a deep, smouldering resentment that was not going to go away and which threatened to haunt the pair of them for the rest of their lives. Now, just when he thought that his false friend had gone into permanent hibernation he erupted again. And here he was. It was all simplicity itself yet complex beyond belief.

'Sit down, do,' said Carpenter. 'Make yourself at home. Can I get you anything?'

'Thank you, no,' said Tudor.

'You're looking well. I enjoyed your drone on Pirates. Picked it up on closed circuit TV. For various reasons I'm not leaving the cabin or I'd have come and attended in person.

Very professional. Like the way you wander about. And good work with the hand-mike. Very practised.'

'Thank you very much.' Tudor inclined his head. 'So to what do we owe this unexpected pleasure?'

Ashley smiled a smug superior smile.

'Well,' he said, 'it's a long story, but it all arose out of my visiting fellowship at this really quite bizarre university. It's not like any other academic institution I've been associated with. Very liberating. Not conventional at all. We teach traditional subjects and disciplines but in a non-traditional way. For example, the old-fashioned notion that the teachers are in some way 'in charge' of the students — that's out of the window. It's a true democracy. Like I say, very liberating.'

'So you thought you'd do some liberating beyond the college walls?'

Ashley laughed though he didn't seem to find the remark particularly funny.

'I have to admit that knowing that you and Elizabeth were on board gave the idea an extra piquancy, but liberating the *Duchess* seemed a perfect idea. She's both marvellously high-profile and incredibly vulnerable. The easiest possible target but also the most headline-grabbing.'

'But plan A didn't work?'

'Evidently not,' said Ashley, 'though there was always an element of fantasy in that, don't you think? It was always unlikely that our gallant little band would actually take the ship over and I'm delighted that you were able to call their bluff. It should prove a thoroughly educational experience for the children. I trust they'll learn from it. But I always thought Plan B was more likely to be successful. As indeed appears to be the case.'

He did look intolerably smug, thought Tudor. He had never seemed smug at Oxford. Rather the reverse. Perhaps, however, that apparent callowness had really been an inferiority complex that he and others had been too insensitive to recognize. Maybe the English of that generation had seemed insufferable. Maybe they had inflicted humiliations without quite knowing that they were doing so. He had not consciously felt arrogant at the time but perhaps that was how he had looked.

It was all immaterial anyway. The harm was done and he was now, in mid-life, lumbered with a stalker of alarming ingenuity and determination.

'What about Sam Hardy?'

'Sam?' repeated Carpenter in an absurdly conversational way as if they were making tea-time small talk and Tudor had just asked about one of the neighbours.

'Sam's fine,' he said.

'Then where is he? He's not here. He's supposed to have laryngitis.'

'Alas poor Sam!' murmured Ashley, pressing the ends of his fingers together and closing his eyes as if in deep contemplation. 'So very greedy when it came down to it. They say everyone has his price but even so.'

'Is he OK?' Tudor did not wish the Master dead.

'He's fine, like I said. A distinguished guest on our floating campus somewhere over there on the ocean deep. Doesn't have his gold, of course, though there was never any question of his being allowed to keep that.'

'And you,' said Tudor. 'What about you? I don't get it. I just don't understand.'

'You never did,' said Ashley abruptly. 'I'm another story altogether.' He glanced at his watch. 'We have plenty of time so I'll tell you some of it. Not all, mind. We need to retain a few surprises up our sleeve, don't you agree?'

26

'Once upon a time,' said Ashley, 'or should I ask if you're sitting comfortably? Or are both those gambits too patronizing for you?'

'Just get on with it,' said Tudor. He disliked being played with and if this was a cat and mouse situation he didn't honestly see that Ashley was entitled to the cat position. He himself had at least as many shots left in his locker, didn't he?

'Actually I think I'll start at the end and work backwards,' said Ashley. 'You could say that the early history is water under the bridge, or that we've drawn a line under it — except, of course, that I don't suppose I ever shall. But let us for the time being concern ourselves with the here and now.'

'Let's,' said Tudor sharply. The cabin creaked.

'Sam Hardy first then. Sam is, as you know, something of a joke. However passengers seem to love him and he does the Jolly Jack Tar bit to the manner born. He remains, as far as Riviera are concerned, an asset even though everyone, most of all Sam, knows that the asset is dwindling. He is a certain age; he is a little too fond of pink gins — made always, as you know with Plymouth full strength, the angostura left in and just a splash of still Malvern. No ice. Definitely no ice. Sam's pension arrangements are dodgy to non-existent and when offered the opportunity of jumping ship with several million pounds worth of gold ingots I'm afraid he needed distressingly little persuasion.

'I — we — were able to offer him the bolt hole he needed and which otherwise he would never have secured. Who knows, he might even have been able to hang onto the gold if your friend Mr Rayner hadn't so disobligingly and unexpectedly heaved into view aboard his wretched *Clipper*.'

'That was bad luck.'

'Yes,' agreed Ashley, 'very. But by then Sam was safely on board our vessel and I had swapped places and was ensconced in his very comfortable quarters aboard the *Duchess*.'

'So,' said Tudor, 'things weren't going to plan.'

'Not to plan A perhaps,' agreed Ashley, 'but I was still happy that we were more or less adhering to plan B. Maureen, the *soi-disant* editor of the *Tipperary Tatler* whom you now know quite well had mercifully broken out from the brig and was a valuable aide, disguised in one of my friend Abdullah's wives' voluminous robes. And we were only a few days out from New York where we could, indeed can, be guaranteed an enthusiastic welcome from the likes of Senator Kennedy and his followers. You simply can't underestimate the strength of the Irish lobby in the States and when a certain sort of feisty Irish band cocks a snook at the former Imperial power then you're on to a certain winner. It might have been better to have managed the take-over of the *Duchess* in mid-Atlantic but there would have been complications — after all what were we to do with several hundred elderly Brits in corsets and on zimmers? In New York they can simply be wheeled ashore while we enjoy day upon day of singular propaganda scoop.'

'But you'll be arrested by the American authorities. There'll be a trial. You haven't a hope.'

'Don't worry your tiny head on that subject,' said Ashley. 'The ground has been well prepared. In any case what exactly would we be tried for?'

'Hang on,' said Tudor, 'let's go back to Sam for a second. What's his part in all this?'

'Sam's what you might call a stool-pigeon or a stalking horse. I'm not sure. Your command of arcane idiom was always so much greater than mine. Just one reason I hated you so much. Sam, a victim of his own blind greed, is now as it were a visiting fellow aboard our hall-of-residence at sea. As such you could say that he is a sort of hostage. Were anyone to attempt anything desperate with relation to the *Duchess* then Sam might suffer. Riviera Shipping might not mind that, but they'd hate the publicity. Why would anyone want to put their trust and their life's savings at the disposal of a company which allowed their most illustrious sea captain to be abducted on the high seas and then, as it were, be thrown to the sharks, walk the plank, or whatever? Again, you're the one with the idiom. Write your own metaphor.'

'So Sam is being held against his will? He's effectively been kidnapped.'

Ashley smiled.

'It's a nice point isn't it? Sam left the *Duchess* quite voluntarily with several million pounds in gold. He boarded our vessel entirely of his own accord and without any coercion because he believed that we could guarantee him and his loot a safe haven. So in that sense and up to that point I plead innocence. It is conceivable that now Sam, having lost his ill-gotten gains, may be having second thoughts. Difficult to say and even more difficult to prove. Eventually, I dare say, he'll be put ashore to face whatever music lies in store. For the time being, however, he remains afloat where he may conceivably be of use to me and mine as a sort of bargaining tool, guarantee, call him what you will.'

'Hostage,' ventured Tudor.

'I'd rather not use that word. It carries mildly pejorative undertones. Not appropriate.'

'So that's Sam Hardy.'

'Yes,' said Ashley, 'that's Sam Hardy. I'm sorry about Mandy Goldslinger. She's distraught, I understand, and the truth may prove even more unpalatable. Sam has rather let her down She won't like it. Woman scorned and all that. I wouldn't want to get the wrong side of La Goldslinger.'

'No,' Tudor agreed. 'And the others?'

'Watkyn's working for MI6 and Grim for 5. But, of course you knew that.'

'Of course,' Tudor lied. The information actually came as rather a shock. He had put both men down as ineffectual independents. All, piss and wind. Maybe they still were but it sounded as if they had official backing which made them more of a force to be reckoned with. Though perhaps 'force' was the wrong word.

'Watkyn's Six and Grim's Five,' said Tudor. 'Are you sure that's right?'

'Five, Six, who cares?' asked Ashley rhetorically. 'Both as useless as each other. The umbrella description is 'security services' or something like that, but whatever you call them they're no bloody good. Loada wankers.'

'You're telling me that Watkyn and Grim work for the British security services?'

Ashley shrugged and smiled. 'Same way Goldslinger works for the CIA. *Work* is pitching it a bit high. Security is clearly a misnomer. Nevertheless and up to a point, well, yes. Though I'm never sure whether Watkyn works for Six and Grim for Five or vice versa. Six is the flaky upmarket FCO one and five the working class nitty-gritty Home Office equivalent so I think I'm right. Could be wrong. The name of the game, after all, is bluff, counter bluff, triple bluff and bluff *ad infinitum*. Ask John le Carré — he worked for both. Then invented his own. He was right. It's a never-never land that one makes up as one goes along. You know that as well as I do.'

'Yes,' said Tudor, bridling. 'Well.'

'And, of course, Mandy Goldslinger is CIA.'

'Now you are fantasizing,' said Tudor irritably, 'she'll be upset about Sam but if she's a CIA agent then the Pope's the King of Swaziland.'

'You don't know that,' said Ashley, 'about Goldslinger. I buy what you say about the Pope and His Majesty the King of Swaziland, but now I've sown a seed about Goldslinger you'll never be absolutely a hundred per cent sure about her. That's the wonderful thing about sowing seeds. No smoke without fire. I'm not suggesting that your friend Mandy is a very important cog in the American Intelligence wheel but I most certainly think she's not above an expensive meal with some chap from the Grosvenor Square Embassy and that she's quite happy to betray little confidences for a couple of dry martinis and a *filet mignon*. Way of the world. Wouldn't you agree?'

In a sense and up to a fashion Tudor did. Uncertainty and innuendo were oxygen in the world of espionage, and espionage certainly came within the ambit of his department. Why else would he be lobbying so hard for an Honorary Doctorate for John le Carré?

'You're mad,' he said, sensing that attack was the best form of defence, if not always at least where Ashley Carpenter was concerned.

'Oddly enough,' said Ashley, 'you're by no means the first person to say that. Little Elizabeth used to say it often. It's a question of definition I suppose but, mad certainly isn't the word I'd use. Obsessed or obsessive might be nearer the mark and possibly even something I'd admit to. Mad is very loose. Byron mad? I don't think so; 'bad and dangerous to know' rather more plausible. I think mad is too often just a loose term of abuse. That's the way you're using it. You're just calling me mad because I'm on your back and you can't shake me off. Furthermore you don't understand what's going on so you're flailing around and seeking to explain things by branding me mad. I'm profoundly unconvinced.'

And he made a pyramid of his palms and rested his chin on the fingertips.

'Smug bastard,' thought Tudor, but also mad as the proverbial hatter.

Out loud he said, 'I don't think any court of law would find you completely sane. And you're certainly not rational.'

'Oh Tudor, Tudor,' said Ashley acting exasperated. 'You're so conventional and English. Who in their right mind would wish to be found sane by a court of law? The very idea.'

He laughed. Tudor thought the laugh manic but, as he conceded ruefully, he would, wouldn't he?

'OK,' said Tudor, 'let's cut out the verbiage and introspection. What happens now?'

Ashley appeared to contemplate for a

while, as if he was thinking about his plans for the first time. Then he said, 'What would you do in my position? And what would you *like* me to do?'

'Never answer a question with a question,' said Tudor repeating a mantra he had learned at his first boarding-school or even perhaps, though he would never dare mention it, from a nanny or governess. More cause for resentment.

'Masterly inactivity,' said Ashley. 'There has been too much action for one transatlantic crossing so for the remainder of the voyage we shall do as little as possible.'

'And when we dock . . . ?'

'Ah,' said Ashley complacently, 'then activity will resume. We shall disembark most but not all the passengers. Most of the crew will remain on board. I shall tell the authorities that you and your accomplice, well, maybe we should extend the focus of our accusation to include more than just little Miss Burney, and include one or two other players such as the Umlauts perhaps, or even your friend Mandy Goldslinger, that you and yours have been involved.'

'Have been *what*?' Tudor was incredulous. 'You *are* mad. No one is going to believe you.'

'On the contrary, dear boy. In today's 'war on terrorism' people will believe what they want to believe. I have friends in the requisite high places, including the press and television. The basic tale will be that, together with my trusty band of free spirits, I have foiled a plot, fiendishly conjured up by your good self, to commandeer one of the most famous ships in the world and use her for your own nefarious ends.'

'But that's crazy,' said Tudor, 'that's what *you* were attempting. Not me. You're standing reality on its head.'

'In a manner of speaking,' conceded Ashley, 'but mirror images are what so much of life is about, don't you think? You have made yourself believe that I am the fruitcake determined on a desperate bid to hijack the *Duchess*, hold the Master to ransom and so on and so forth. But why not you, pray? Why should you be presumed innocent? I should add, incidentally, that I have been busy sowing seeds. The American authorities and my friends in high places are prepared for something much like this. There has been a whispering campaign. Tip-offs. As soon as we reach New York they will be ready and waiting. You will be surprised at the extent of documentary evidence. Convincing stuff, if I say so myself.'

He sat back and smirked.

Tudor was unnerved and would have been

more so had he not known, or at least suspected, that he was privy to information which Ashley was not. Even so he felt chilled.

27

Sea and sky were grey and sullen and would have seemed threatening and filled with menace were it not such a relief to escape his enemy's presence.

Elizabeth was leaning over the rail on the helicopter deck gazing out at the two widening white lines of wash behind them. She seemed pensive.

'The Master is on the *Michael Collins*,' he said, 'somewhere out there.' And he gestured at the huge anonymity of the sea.

'Are you sure?' she asked, not unreasonably. 'How do you know? Where have you been? People have been looking for you.'

'That's what I'm about to tell you,' he said. 'Sam Hardy and Mr X have done a swap. The mystery guest is in Sam's cabin waiting to pounce. Guess who?'

'I hate silly games,' she said. 'Tell me.'

He told her.

'That's so surprising it's not surprising,' she said. 'I was half expecting him.'

'You didn't know anything?'

'Of course not.' She seemed mildly irritated. 'Ashley's past history as far as I'm concerned. Not you though. Not by the sound of it. Why's he here? Just to make trouble for you?'

'That, and I don't know . . . I think he's flipped. I mean this bogus sounding so-called Irish university and their floating campus. I think they've gone to his head, infected his brain. I actually think he sees himself as some sort of latter day Che Guevara. I'm not joking. He believes his own publicity, thinks he can change the world. There are people like that.'

'Mostly writing columns for the *Daily Mail*,' said Elizabeth sharply. 'I'm not convinced academics and others should try too much real world stuff. I've just been having a chat with Major Timbers.'

'Oh him,' said Tudor, 'I'd forgotten about him.'

This was true. Tudor found the Major instantly forgettable. This was true of most majors.

'I think he's quite fanciable, if you like that sort of thing.'

'And do you?'

'I might.' There was a glint in her eye. She was only doing it to tease.

'The Major is a great one for men and boys, chaps staying out of the kitchen if they can't stand the heat, leave it all to the professionals, *sang-froid*, gung-ho, stiff upper-lip, straight bat and when the chips are down the Brits do this sort of thing supremely well.'

'And you believe him?'

'Not really,' she smiled. 'On the other hand I was hoping this would be a quiet crossing and we could all relax. That's what he said: 'Just relax and go with the flow'.'

'He said that?'

'His very words.'

'He thinks he has everything under control?'

'That's what he said.'

'That sort of person always says that sort of thing,' said Tudor. 'They said it before the Fall of Singapore. You know, 'Don't worry our men are supremely well prepared and the Japanese can't see in the dark'.'

'And 'don't like it up 'em, Captain Mainwaring'.'

'Precisely,' said Tudor. 'False optimism; whistling in the dark, a Dickensian 'something will turn up' characteristic of the British middle-classes. Something always does turn up in my experience, but seldom what you expect.'

'It was men like Major Timbers who won the war,' said Elizabeth. 'They made Britain great. My father always told me so. All phlegm, grit and stoicism.'

'All moustache and no chin,' said Tudor, 'they're what makes Britain mediocre.'

'You should know,' said Elizabeth. The remark seemed meaningless since Tudor was clean-shaven and had a jaw which did not exactly jut but was a jaw nonetheless, but it was intended to be hurtful. Tudor was duly hurt. He felt vulnerable and unwanted.

'I think people like the Major are a menace,' he said with feeling. 'They're second-rate to the core, but they get away with murder because in some unexplained way they are able to pass themselves off as 'Players' whereas they're 'Gentlemen'. I grant you that there used to be a caricature of brilliant amateur detectives and plodding professional policemen which was unfair to the police but the pendulum has swung too far the other way. You won't find brilliance or intuition among the boys in blue and sometimes you find pedestrianism and downright incompetence. If the shenanigans on board ship were left to plodders like the Major nothing would ever be solved.'

As if to add credence to this judgement the bardic figure of Sir Goronwy Watkyn came into view walking with exaggeratedly bowed legs as if to tell the rest of those on board that he was, among many other things, a salty old sea-dog of great experience. He shook his shaggy locks in Tudor's direction and said, 'Been warned off by the acting skipper. Little Grim likewise. A diabolical liberty. Crime occurs and you have real experts on hand with none of the concomitant obstruction of the local constabulary and you don't just ignore what we have to offer — you positively shackle it. Outrageous.'

With his low opinion of Watkyn and Grim, Tudor was inclined to side with Angus Donaldson, but at the same time he recognized that a strike against them was part of a strike against himself as well.

'And another thing.' The old Welshman looked as if he had a long list of 'other things' about which to complain. 'Bloody Donaldson seems to have stopped talking to the ship from the bridge. No noon message. What's more the chart showing the ship's progress hasn't been updated. According to what's on it we haven't moved at all for at least forty-eight hours.' He peered out into the murky gloom. 'We could be absolutely any bloody where. I shall complain to my agent when we get home.'

Tudor thought privately that this was a threat unlikely to alarm Riviera Shipping. He also noted that if the old boy was correct about the captain's non-speak regarding the ship's position it served to confirm his innermost suspicions and make his letter to Donaldson all the more worthwhile.

'He must be under a lot of strain with the Master's laryngitis and everything.'

'Laryngitis, my arse,' said Sir Goronwy. 'Believe that and you'll believe Wales have a half-decent football team. Sam Hardy's no more got laryngitis than I have. The day he loses his voice will be the day I lose mine.'

The thought of Goronwy Watkyn losing his voice was indeed preposterous. Some sort of plastic container floated into the wake and bobbed about for a while reminding them all of man's threat to the world. There was no sign of fish nor fowl, just the *Duchess* and hundreds of humans.

'We could be anywhere,' said Watkyn gloomily, 'and I'm not at all convinced Donaldson and his people know what they're about. That Major Wood is all piss and wind. I'm not happy about the Abdullah cove nor the Umlaut dwarfs. Neither up to any good. And someone must have dropped a fire-cracker in the Krauts' crêpes Suzettes last night. One of the Prince's wives if you ask me. I noticed one stroll past just before the conflagration. And what's happened to the Irish press party? Haven't had sight nor sound for days now. All passed out down below somewhere, I suppose. And the other morning we seemed to have some sort of emergency and then we don't have an emergency.'

'It was a drill,' lied Tudor, 'not a real emergency. A fake.'

'Huh!' Sir Goronwy cleared his throat emphysematically. 'I shall be glad to be back in the Land of My Fathers. I usually enjoy these trips but present company excepted this has been a bit of a downer. Haven't even sold many books. And there's something badly wrong somewhere. I feel it in my water. Talking of which would anyone care for a snifter. The drink of the day's negroni.'

The trio tottered off to the Rum Locker a small sepulchral bar which had somehow missed out on the usual stately home nomenclature and had passable negronis mixed by Klaus, a middle-aged, strawberry-nosed bartender from Dresden who had been with the ship since her maiden voyage. Nothing significant was said over this drink which presently blurred into a second and was followed by food and more drink and by more drink and more food and by a little bit of lying down and a little bit of walking around the promenade deck and a snooze in the cinema and tea and sandwiches and a look in on the bingo and a rehearsal of the dance troupe and an abortive shop, not knowing whether or not to invest in some duty-free which would probably be cheaper in Tesco in Casterbridge, and a bit of a lie-down and a shower and another stroll and a perusal of the evening's menu and a spin through the old movies on the stateroom TV and an attempt at reading an H.R.F. Keating 'Inspector Ghote' mystery spoiled with the sudden realization that it had been read already and one knew whodunit and a nodding off while lying down and a changing for dinner and, in short, all the little procrastinations and indulgences of a day at sea aboard the *Duchess*.

Yet for Tudor it was not just a typical day at sea for he was all too aware of his *bête noire*'s presence, usurper of the Captain's cabin, determined apparently to destroy his life but slowly, stealthily, twisting the knife gently. Carpenter was not interested in a quick kill. Tudor guessed that Ashley would like him arrested, maybe even tried, but would prefer to have him released so that he could resume the slow torture.

And yet was the whole elaborate scheme really just another piece of slowly savoured revenge? Sam Hardy must have been a willing thief motivated, surely, by greed, not any feelings towards Tudor. Relations between the two men had always been cordial. Or had they? And the Prince and his harem. And the Umlauts. Little Grim. Ambrose Perry the gentleman host. Mandy Goldslinger. Donaldson. He knew he was being paranoid and yet when did justified suspicion shade into neurosis?

Whenever he almost lost himself in food, drink, slumber, ambling or some spectator sport Tudor found himself shaken back into suspicion and fear. He should, by now, be relaxed and euphoric but instead he was a seething mess of worry and nerves. Every time he saw a woman in concealing robes he found himself shivering with apprehension. He flinched whenever there was a gastronomic combustion in the Chatsworth Restaurant. He searched for a hidden meaning whenever anyone addressed him, even if it was Waclav or Natalia asking if he would like the prawn cocktail or the chicken liver parfait. The pop of a champagne cork made him jump. He saw stalkers in the shadows on deck.

In bed, he slept but did not sleep. He tried reading and failed. He counted sheep and failed at that too. He played tic-tac-toe with Elizabeth but found it impossible to concentrate. He reviewed his life and his achievements, decided that he was an abject failure, that every crucial decision had been a wrong one, that he should never have been an academic, should never have specialized in Criminal Affairs and, perhaps most particularly, he should never have met Ashley Carpenter much less befriended him.

Not for the first time in the last few years and, he feared, not for the last, he cudgelled his mind for memories of Carpenter. Was it a girl? Was it something to do with rowing? Or their studies? Had something happened in a tutorial? Or was it life after university? Did this enmity hinge on later life? What was it? What possible slight or injustice could have triggered such an obsessive hatred? Or was he imagining the entire feud?

At last, alone, he turned out the light and saw that the sky had cleared and a full moon shone pale on an ink-black sea. There were no whitecaps — only a gentle roll and swell which made the old ship creak and sway. The rhythms and sounds usually soothed him to sleep, but tonight every movement and every noise triggered a nervy response, a sudden sitting-up in bed, a pad to the lavatory, a sip of water, a mop of brow, another fruitless attempt at memory.

Try as he might he slept only in fits and starts, woken even by his own soft snoring. He was a wreck.

28

He must have dozed off though he would later deny it. At first he thought his snoring had woken him again, but then he realized that the noise came from outside. Even through his waking wooziness he recognized it immediately: helicopter. He hurried to the porthole and stared out. The night was clear and away on the horizon he could see flickering lights which must have been on the shore. His stateroom was on the port-side. That could mean only one thing. He was right. Close to the ship the bulbous shape of a big whirly-bird hovered alongside. She looked like a Puma but in all honesty he knew very little about helicopters. He suspected she came from Culdrose near Helston in Cornwall, the biggest helicopter station in Europe. That was if his supposition was correct. In any event, if he was right, it was one of ours.

He glanced at his watch. It said 4 a.m. though they had been through so many time changes announced and unannounced that the information might have meant anything. The point was that it was still dark though there was just a hint of light at the edges of the picture before him.

Behind him the bedside phone shrilled. He picked it up and heard a clipped English voice say, 'Dr Cornwall, sir. Captain Donaldson presents his compliments and would be pleased if you could present yourself as soon as possible at the helicopter landing pad on Boat Deck.'

It was on the tip of his tongue to reply 'Aye, aye, sir', but it was not in Tudor's nature to be flippant, particularly at times like this which was not just the middle of the night but crucial in the unfolding of the convoluted drama of the past few days. Or so he assumed. The phone sounded again. This time it was Elizabeth.

'Is that a helicopter?' she asked fatuously. Tudor excused her on the grounds of her obvious sleepiness.

'Landing imminent he said,' he said. 'Donaldson has been kind enough to invite me to help greet her despite his warning me off. I suggest you join us if you want a bit of excitement or interest at least.'

'Is it American?' she asked, not unreasonably.

'I'd be very surprised,' he said, 'but I'll see you up there and explain then.' Saying which he replaced the receiver, pulled on a woollen rollneck, corduroy trousers and a pair of desert boots, ran a comb through his hair, grimaced at his pouchy eyes and designer stubble, put his room card key in his pocket and hurried out almost colliding with a be-jeaned and fleece-topped Elizabeth in the corridor outside.

'I don't understand,' she said.

'If I'm right,' he said, as they waited for the elevator in the foyer by one of the endless gift shoppes on board, 'we're in British territorial waters and Detective Chief Superintendent Eddie Trythall of the Wessex Constabulary is about to take over the investigation.'

The lift-doors slid open, they got in and Tudor pressed the Boat Deck button.

'But,' she protested, 'we should be taking on the New York pilot somewhere around the Nantucket light.'

'*Should* doesn't come into it,' he said. 'If I'm right Donaldson and his crew turned the ship round and hardly anyone noticed.'

'Huh?' she said, still drowsy. This information was clearly too much to assimilate.

'In a few hours' time, if I'm right, we'll be tying up alongside the quay at Budmouth,' he said, as the doors slid open on to the Boat Deck foyer.

'What makes you think that?' she asked, rubbing sleep from her eyes and yawning.

'The sun rises in the east and sets in the west, yes?'

'I suppose,' she said. 'Geography was never my strong point. Or is it astrology. Red sky in the morning, shepherd's warning; red sky at night, shepherd's delight. That's about as much as I can do on dawns and dusks.'

'Trust me,' said Tudor. 'So when you came back down and said you'd just seen the most exquisite sunrise over the bows I put two and two together.'

They pushed through a heavy door out on to the open deck and heard the thudding metallic clatter of the chopper low overhead. The blades were creating a heavy down-draught like a mechanical whirlwind. A little knot of officers standing on the edge of the helipad was literally holding on to its collective hat. Donaldson was among them and seeing Tudor and the girl managed something almost resembling a smile.

'Got your letter, Doctor,' he shouted, over the wind and rattle of the helicopter, 'and passed it on to my Board. They seem to take a more, shall we say, lateral view of procedures than I sometimes do myself. If I'm not much mistaken your man is on board.'

'Good. Thank you,' said Tudor, 'and congratulations. It was clever to turn her round with no one noticing.'

'Aye,' said Donaldson, looking momen-
tarily pleased with himself in a monosyllabic
Fife fashion, 'the weather was on our side. So
overcast and grey you couldn't make out any
features at all. Could have been anywhere.'

'Except for one dawn.'

'Didn't last long,' said the acting Captain.

'Long enough.'

'Happen.'

'She's coming down, sir,' said one of the
younger officers whom Tudor had never seen
before. He noticed Major Timbers in a
dark-blue track suit. He looked muscular and
menacing in the gloom. Tudor doubted his
mental capacity but not his combat skills. He
looked as if he could kill with his bare hands
— not something to which Tudor aspired.

The onlookers backed against the wall of
what, in agreeable weather, did service as a
Lido Bar, called, since this was, after all, the
good ship *Duchess*, the Croquet Lawn. It did
a good line in Pimms of various otherwise
forgotten varieties. There was even an
Imperial one using brandy and champagne. It
seemed a long way away as the helicopter
throbbed slowly deckward, swayed once or
twice and then hit the surface, bounced
almost imperceptibly and came to a halt. The
pilot cut the engine and the blades turned

slower and slower before eventually coming to a full stop. There was a short pause, then a door slid open and a burly figure in a belted trench coat and tweed cap stepped with surprising agility on the deck of the *Duchess*. Eddie Trythall of the Wessex Constabulary.

Donaldson went forward to greet him. 'Chief Superintendent Trythall I presume,' he said, and the two shook hands perfunctorily. Then, almost at once, the policeman spotted and recognized the academic, his lifelong sparring partner. The two had known each other almost as long as Ashley and Tudor. Their mutual respect might have been grudging but it was at least genuine. As was their affection.

'Doctor!' said Trythall. 'Got your message. Let me deploy these men — with the permission and assistance of the Master, of course,' he added, recognizing that proprieties had to be observed even though there was no technical need and even though he wanted to listen to what Tudor had to say far more than he wanted to have his ear bent by a Merchant Navy captain from Anstruther, no matter how seamanlike he might be.

For a few moments he and Donaldson engaged in an earnest confabulation. Then Major Timbers was summoned and evidently co-opted into some sort of liaison role involving Trythall's policemen who, Tudor was impressed to see, appeared to be heavily armed, to be wearing flak jackets and to be accompanied by two enormous German Shepherd dogs. He almost felt sorry for the girl called *Tipperary Tatler*, for Professor Carpenter, the Prince and his harem, and anyone else who looked like getting in the way of the forces of conventional law and order.

Presently this conference was over; men were deployed; and the police gave every indication of behaving with their customary efficiency. It was not a pretty sight, nor marked by the sort of intellectual rigour Dr Cornwall prided himself on displaying on campus. Despite this — perhaps because of it — the effect was scary. You wouldn't want to get on the wrong side of this lot.

'Now,' said Eddie, rubbing his hands and blowing into the cold night air. 'Time for a nice hot cup of tea and a quiet chat.' He stared meaningfully at Major Timbers, at Elizabeth, at Angus Donaldson, and added with quiet menace. 'With my old friend Dr Cornwall. In private.' There was a pause which might properly have been described as pregnant and even ugly but which flattened out into an almost deferential acquiescence. Donaldson instructed a Filipino steward to take the policeman and the detective down to the wardroom while everyone else peeled off.

This officers' day-room which, thankfully, paid not even lip-service to the prevailing theme of 'dead *Duchess* upstairs' but was dominated by a large photograph of a youngish Queen Elizabeth II and several dozen shields presented by other ships from around the world as well as ports where the *Duchess* had at one time or another been made welcome. Inside, the Chief Superintendent removed his cap and coat, sat down heavily on a leatherette sofa and said, laughing, 'Well this is a turn-up for the book, old son.'

'You could say that,' agreed Tudor. 'It's good to see you. They wouldn't pay much attention to me even though I think I've got the whole thing more or less wrapped up. If there are any uncrossed 't's' or undotted 'i's' I'm sure that between us we can do the necessary.'

Tea, hot, sweet, rough Indian and quite unlike the refined stuff served in the passenger areas, arrived in short order together with digestive biscuits. Trythall dunked one in his mug and said, 'One stroke of luck was that we had a frigate in mid-Atlantic. HMS *Truro*. She happened to be passing when we had a mildly alarming message from our friend Rayner aboard the *Star Clipper*. As a result I'm happy to say that the not-so-good-ship *Michael Collins* was boarded by a party from the Special Boat Service and Captain Sam Hardy was discovered tied up and indubitably being held against his will. He was not a happy bunny. I have to say that the ship shows every sign of failing every known regulation regarding health and safety at sea. She's being escorted to Falmouth by the *Truro*. Against all the rules, of course, but frankly there's bugger all anyone can do about it.'

'Captain Sam went aboard of his own accord,' said Tudor. 'He was hoping to make off with several million pounds worth of gold ingots.'

The Chief Superintendent dunked more biscuit.

'I have a feeling that might complicate our case,' he said. 'I see no very good reason why Captain Sam shouldn't have been abducted against his will by these obvious terrorists. It's in everyone's interests for him to look like a really good guy, wouldn't you say?'

'Certainly simpler,' said Tudor.

'Yes, well. That's my news. What's yours?'

So Tudor told him about the Irish take-over bid; how it was foiled; how Ashley Carpenter had come on board; how the *Tipperary*

Tatler girl had disguised herself as one of the Prince's brides and incinerated the Umlauts; how the Prince and the Umlauts were at daggers drawn in their ambitions to gain control of the ship albeit, as far as he could judge, by more or less legal boardroom means; how that old windbag Goronwy Watkyn had tried to get in on the act and that slimy little creep Freddie Grim, whom they both remembered from his days in the Met. And how he had serious reservations about a gentleman's host called Ambrose Perry but suspected that he was guilty of nothing much worse than battening on elderly ladies who liked to believe that they were doing the rhumba with him. And how he had a soft spot for Mandy Goldslinger even though her infatuation with Captain Sam was remarkably silly. That, of course, didn't make her a criminal. Far from it in fact. She was actually rather gullible and for all her Lauren Bacall affectations a bit of an ingénue.

Detective Chief Superintendent Trythall listened to this baroque tale with a half-smile playing around his tea-wettened, biscuit-crumbed lips and eventually said, 'It looks as if your old mate Professor Carpenter has given himself enough rope to hang himself with. I don't know what the rest of his gang will get. Time off for gullibility, I should think. But the case against Carpenter strikes me as cast-iron, watertight. We should be able to get him off your back for a good many years.'

'You reckon?' Tudor was dubious, 'He'll get the best possible defence lawyers if he doesn't conduct his own case. Which would probably help us. He's brilliant at wriggling out of impossible situations. He's done it before and I have a horrible feeling he'll do it again.'

'Don't see how he can manage it this time,' said Trythall. 'And if we go easy on everyone else we should be able to find plenty of witnesses to testify against him.'

He paused and drank some sweet tea.

'Even so,' he said, 'I don't fully understand this obsession. How come he hates you so much? It's not rational.'

'No,' said Tudor, shaking his head with disbelief. 'He used to be my best friend. At least I thought he was.'

'That's the problem then,' said Eddie. 'Like the marriage partner who thinks they've been wronged; you must have been too close.'

'I suppose,' said Tudor. 'I hope we can have him sent down for a long spell in clink but I have an unpleasant feeling he'll be back. He's a man obsessed. A little thing like prison won't put him off.'

With which thought they sat and contemplated the remains of their tea. Outside the wind started to sigh and the old ship pitched and rolled as if in one final dismissive nautical V-sign before reaching the haven of her home port.

★   ★   ★

A day after docking, Elizabeth and Tudor shared a bottle of vintage Bitschwiller in Henchards wine bar and conducted a desultory post-mortem.

Donaldson's role bothered him.

On the face of it he was dour, unimaginative and honest as the day was long. Tudor doubted whether he had the wit to be a real villain even if the temptation existed. The trouble was that here on board ship an investigator's hands were tied in a way that they would not be on dry land. He was reminded of a famous radio interview involving the Glaswegian comic Billy Connolly. Before the interview Connolly had negotiated a deal in which no questions would be asked about his then girlfriend. However, the second the programme went live on-air the interviewer asked, 'What about your girlfriend, Billy?' Instead of responding angrily Connolly remained utterly silent and continued to do so in the face of every further question. The result of this tactic was that after a while the audience refused to believe that Connolly was in the studio. It was a stunning example of the efficacy of silence.

On dry land, Tudor's friend Trythall would have the power to insist on a response. There were safeguards, of course: the presence of lawyers, the necessity of cautions but, essentially, someone like Trythall had the force of law on his side, and a powerful apparatus to enable him to determine what was true and what was false. And because Tudor had worked on his contacts and established confidence and trust, people like Trythall confided in him.

None of this applied on board ship. If, as he had done, Donaldson refused to accept Dr Cornwall's status or even competence, he was perfectly able to do so. Tudor's hands were effectively tied. He could not, for instance, believe that the changing of locks on the door of the Captain's cabin would have been something Donaldson would have been ignorant of even if he had not initiated it. But if Donaldson said that, in effect, it was none of Tudor's business then Tudor had, perforce to accept what Donaldson decreed. In the Master's absence he, Donaldson, was in charge. Back in port it would be different.

Donaldson would be questioned and he would answer. It was to his credit that he had voluntarily and possibly at some risk steered his ship back into an area of British jurisdiction. This would tell in his favour. But until then Tudor was an impotent innocent.

'My new rule is never to believe that any passenger ship will necessarily arrive at the destination advertised,' said Tudor. 'Rule for life too. Don't expect to arrive where you expect when you begin your journey. That way disappointment lies.'

Elizabeth sipped her Bitschwiller thoughtfully. 'Mine's simpler,' she smiled, contemplating the leisurely bead of the amber liquid. She fixed her boss with luminous eyes.

'Never,' she said, 'believe anything you are told by a guest lecturer.'

We do hope that you have enjoyed reading this large print book.

Did you know that all of our titles are available for purchase?

We publish a wide range of high quality large print books including:
Romances, Mysteries, Classics
General Fiction
Non Fiction and Westerns

Special interest titles available in large print are:
The Little Oxford Dictionary
Music Book
Song Book
Hymn Book
Service Book

Also available from us courtesy of Oxford University Press:
Young Readers' Dictionary
(large print edition)
Young Readers' Thesaurus
(large print edition)

For further information or a free brochure, please contact us at:
Ulverscroft Large Print Books Ltd.,
The Green, Bradgate Road, Anstey,
Leicester, LE7 7FU, England.
Tel: (00 44) 0116 236 4325
Fax: (00 44) 0116 234 0205

AN ACCIDENTAL AMERICAN

Alex Carr

After serving six years in Marseille's toughest prison, Nicole has had enough danger and excitement, and is now living peacefully in the French Pyrenees. But her tranquil life is shattered when John Valsamis turns up wanting her to find her former lover Rahim Ali, regarded by Interpol as a terrorist threat . . . Unable to resist the pull, and wanting to prove Valsamis wrong about Ali, Nicole is persuaded to track him down in Lisbon ahead of a terrorist strike. But as she arrives at Lisbon's Santa Apolonia Station, she realises how foolish her expectations had been . . .

BAD MONKEYS

Matt Ruff

Arrested for murder, Jane Charlotte tells the police that she is a member of 'The Department for the Final Disposition of Irredeemable Persons' — or 'Bad Monkeys' for short. A secret organisation, it's an execution squad that eradicates evil people. But when she kills a man not on the official target list, she is interviewed by the doctor in the psychiatric wing regarding her career as an assassin. Jane's tale grows increasingly bizarre, with dollar bills that can see, and axe-wielding Scary Clowns. Can the truth be unravelled? Is she lying, crazy — or playing a different game altogether . . . ?

HELL'S GATE

Michael Parker

It's 1898 in British East Africa. Reuben Cole finds himself torn between battling to save his son from the evil slave markets of Mombassa and foiling the murderous plans of the exiled Ugandan king, Mwanga. Adding to this torment come the exceptional rains and volcanic disturbances beneath Lake Naivasha, and the threat to the railway camp at Nairobi by 10,000 armed Masai tribesmen. With only 200 soldiers to defend the camp, Major Kingsley Webb faces defeat. Then the lovely Hannah Bowers becomes implicated in the conflict as events pitch Reuben and Kingsley into a struggle for survival — and for Hannah's love . . .

THE RODRIGUEZ AFFAIR

James Pattinson

Harry Banner turns up in London one November evening. Just arrived from Venezuela, he visits Robert Cade, a man he'd known six years earlier in Buenos Aires. Banner wants Cade to keep a certain parcel until he returns for it. But the package remains uncollected: the next morning Banner is found dead in his hotel room, with a stab wound to the chest . . . Other people come looking for the parcel — and Cade departs for Venezuela, intending to investigate Harry's murder. However, in San Borja the climate can be very unhealthy for someone asking too many questions . . .

THE INTERPRETER

Gordon Nimse

In war-torn Burma the Japanese jungle warriors are in full retreat. British agents, weapons and silver rupees cascade from the skies to aid the Karen resistance groups. However, the brutal Japanese Kempetai strike back and double-dealings and split loyalties become the order of the day . . . With the war over and martial retribution taking the stage, peacetime journalist Captain 'Robbie' Roberts insists on defending an Anglo-Burman sergeant accused of waging war against the King. The trial becomes a contest that sensationally brings to light a sinister backdrop of intrigue at the highest level.

THE MOONRAKER MUTINY

Antony Trew

A tired old freighter, the *Moonraker*, is bound from Fremantle to Mauritius. Haunted by his past, Captain Stone seeks solace in the gin bottle in his cabin. His niece, Susie, flirts with Australian passage worker Hank Casey, and Italian mate Carlo Frascatti grumbles at the motley crew. Then the radio operator receives a warning of a suspected cyclone ahead . . . The panic-stricken crew turn on their captain and abandon ship. Those left behind desperately struggle to keep the battered hulk afloat, whilst nearby, a coaster and an ocean salvage tug are each determined to profit from the *Moonraker*'s disaster . . .